Praise for Elle Kennedy's *Midnight Encounters*

"MIDNIGHT ENCOUNTERS had me hooked from beginning to end! ...Elle Kennedy keeps the dialogue fast-paced and moving, making the courtship between these opposites a game of chess: sly, subtle, and sneaky with plenty of intriguing moves on either side. MIDNIGHT ENCOUNTERS started off with a bang and kept going on strong! I highly enjoyed this romance. Elle Kennedy, you've got a new fan!"

~ *Romance Junkies*

"Midnight Encounters was a terrific story that had me smiling all the way through. Elle Kennedy has written a simple love story that is romantic and exciting and a must read for any romance fan."

~ *Fallen Angel Reviews*

Midnight Encounters

Elle Kennedy

A Samhain Publishing, Ltd. publication.

Samhain Publishing, Ltd.
577 Mulberry Street, Suite 1520
Macon, GA 31201
www.samhainpublishing.com

Midnight Encounters
Copyright © 2009 by Elle Kennedy
Print ISBN: 978-1-60504-287-9
Digital ISBN: 1-60504-059-2

Editing by Laurie Rauch
Cover by Tuesday Dube

First Samhain Publishing, Ltd. electronic publication: July 2008
First Samhain Publishing, Ltd. print publication: June 2009

Dedication

To my brilliant editor for having faith in this story...

Chapter One

"Wipe that look off your face, Mags. You'll scare the customers."

Maggie Reilly shoved a wayward strand of wavy red hair off her forehead and glanced at her friend with narrowed eyes. "What look?"

"The *I'm-having-sex-in-an-hour-so-don't-hold-me-up* look." With a cheerful smile, Trisha opened the icebox under the counter and dumped a scoopful of ice cubes into the glass pitcher she was holding.

"Damn and I thought my poker face was solid," Maggie replied with a grin.

Trisha poured ice water into three tall glasses and set them on her black plastic tray. "You'll see your Tony soon enough."

"Who's Tony?" Matthew, the blond bartender, came up behind the two waitresses, curiosity written all over his handsome face.

Maggie shot Trisha a glare that said *one word and I'll kill you.* Aloud, she replied, "No one. Trisha's just screwing around."

Matthew shrugged and headed for the other end of the bar.

"What part of *don't tell anyone* didn't you understand, Trish?" she asked irritably.

The brunette merely gave a shrug of her own. "I don't see what the big deal is. I mean, who doesn't have a Tony in their life? Casual, twice-a-year sex is practically a trend these days."

She ignored her co-worker's remark. Trisha loved teasing her about the arrangement she had with Tony, but Maggie suspected her friend didn't fully understand just how difficult it was for her to maintain a normal love life.

How could she? She spent her afternoons volunteering at the community center, her nights serving drinks here at the Olive Martini. And her nights off? Well, those were reserved for her college classes. So it was really no surprise she'd never found a man willing to accept her hectic schedule. Her boyfriends usually got sick of seeing her only once a month and she'd gotten dumped more times than Elizabeth Taylor's husbands combined.

Not that she was devastated.

Was it her fault men couldn't handle her dedication and work ethic? Growing up dirt poor had made her determined to be successful. She'd struggled to make ends meet all her life, scrimped and saved until she'd been able to pay for her college tuition. In a few short months she'd finally earn her degree in social work, leave the Olive, and hopefully get a permanent—*paying*—position at the community center.

So, really, she didn't need a boyfriend. Of course, that didn't mean she wanted to live like a nun, either, which was precisely why she needed someone like Tony Burke in her life.

Tony was a travel writer who spent eleven and a half months out of the year roaming exotic places and writing about them. He came back to New York usually no more than two or three times a year, and, during one of his visits, Maggie had instantly hit it off with the sexy nomad. They'd wound up in bed the same night they'd met, and their trysts had become somewhat of a routine.

Tony arrived in town, he called her, they had sex. Then they both returned to their bustling lives, sated and content and with no plans to see each other again—until the next time Tony popped up in the city.

She'd last seen him over Christmas, and since it was already May, she'd been expecting him to call any day now. Like clockwork, he had. Just three hours ago, with his hotel room number and the promise of some hot, stress-busting sex.

"Make fun of me all you want, Trish, but we both know you're jealous," she said good-naturedly.

"It's true. I'd give my right arm for a Tony." Trisha made a face. "Instead I have a Lou."

"Aw, be nice. Lou kisses the ground you walk on."

"Yeah, when he's not watching football. Do yourself a favor, Mags. Never date a man who'd rather watch big sweaty goons chase a ball around a field than talk to his girlfriend."

She laughed. Personally, she thought the leggy brunette could do a lot better than Lou Gertz, the high school football coach slash couch potato. But whether Trisha just had bad taste in men, or Lou was a reflection of the kind of guys swimming around in the singles pool, her friend's love life only reaffirmed Maggie's notion that relationships were too much of a hassle. That's why she'd decided to secure her career before she tossed her line into the dating pond and hoped to land a keeper.

"Looks like Tony has some competition," Trisha quipped.

She shifted her gaze and noticed her pot-bellied customer waving at her from across the room. "My biggest fan awaits," she said dryly. "And by the way, he heard you snickering when he commented on my waitressing skills."

Trisha snorted. "He called you a ballerina of the bar. He was asking for a snicker."

"You should have continued eavesdropping. I told him waitress training is extensive and that I had to go through four years of schooling."

As her friend burst into a fit of giggles, Maggie swiped the guy's credit card through the outdated register and waited for the printer to spit out the receipt. She tucked the bill, a pen and some mints inside a sleeve of plastic and then glanced at her watch.

Ten-thirty. God, when was this night going to end? Normally she didn't mind her shifts at the Olive Martini. The job paid her bills, the tips were great, and she couldn't say she didn't have fun. The staff at the Olive was like a big happy family, the customers their interesting—and often completely insane—surrogate children.

But sometimes, no matter how entertaining the crowd was, Maggie just wanted to finish her shift and get the hell out of there.

Tonight was one of those times.

"Again with that look," Trisha chided, wagging her French-manicured finger. "Don't worry, you'll be playing mattress hockey soon enough. I, on the other hand, will be fetching beers for Lou while he makes love to the television."

Maggie's mouth lifted in a grin. "Well, you know what they say—a good Tony is hard to find."

If Ben Barrett saw one more photographer lurking in the bushes, he'd go into cardiac arrest. Or worse, slam his fist into someone's jaw. The latter was so appealing, his palms actually tingled, but he knew as well as anyone how pointless picking a fight would be. The paparazzi would jump all over the story: *Violent Movie Star Assaults Innocent Photographer!*

And then his reputation would take yet another hit, his agent and publicist would freak out, and Ben would be forced to make dozens of morning-talk-show appearances to explain to his fans why he'd knocked someone's lights out.

That's how it always went. You decide to be an actor and you say goodbye to your privacy. Didn't matter that half the stories the tabloids ran were bull. If you left the house with a runny nose, you snorted cocaine. If you had lunch with a male friend, you were gay. If you shoved a photographer out of your face, you had anger problems.

Ben had dealt with this shit for ten years, but that didn't mean he had to like it. Growing up in small-town Iowa, he'd viewed acting as his ticket out of there. He'd never been happier than the day his drama teacher invited a talent agent to one of his performances. But, along with escape, acting had given him a sense of pride. He was good at pretending to be other people, and his first few years in Hollywood were some of the most rewarding of his thirty-two years.

Until, of course, the challenging roles had been replaced with mindless-hero personas, and the public suddenly decided he was nothing more than a toy to play with.

So he'd left. Said *sayonara* to LA and moved to New York, though the Big Apple certainly hadn't been his first choice to lay roots. A house in Colorado or Montana, that's what he'd wanted. A place right up in the mountains, so that if the press wanted to harass him they'd have to work for it. Hiking up a cliff would certainly deter at least half of those nosy bastards.

Of course, his agent balked. With Ben's reputation currently on shaky ground, the worst thing he could do was disappear into some out-of-the-way forest. "If you want to leave Hollywood, fine," his agent had said. "But stay in sight."

So New York it was.

"Hey, aren't you—"

Ben pulled the rim of his Yankees cap lower so that it shielded his face, then bypassed the middle-aged woman who'd just stopped in her tracks and stood there gawking at him. He didn't let her finish her sentence, just hurried along Broadway and tried to disappear in the lively Friday night theater crowd.

Absolutely fucking ridiculous the way he had to skulk around like this, but damn it, he needed some peace and quiet. He'd bought a house on Manhattan's Upper East Side and moved in last week, but had the press left him alone to settle in? No way in hell. They stood on the curb in front of his brownstone day and night, night and day, until Ben wanted to tear every strand of hair from his head.

He hadn't slept in seven days. Hadn't been able to leave the house without being barraged with questions. *Were you with Gretchen the night she died? Did Alan Goodrich know about the affair?*

So many damn questions. He didn't want to deal with them anymore. Or ever. Not when he still hadn't sifted through the emotions he felt over Gretchen's death.

So he'd taken off. Left the house with a trail of media behind him, got in his car and managed to lose the vultures determined to circle over him. He'd ditched his car in the first parking lot he saw, and now he was on foot, in search of the first hotel he could find that had a big bed he could finally fall asleep on.

Now, satisfied that he was rid of every photographer in a ten-mile radius, Ben finally came to a stop in front of the Lester Hotel. He knew there was a Hilton half a dozen blocks away, but he had no intention of checking in there. The Lester, a ten-or-so-story building with a bland gray exterior, was the last place the press would think to look.

Stepping through the revolving door, Ben crossed the empty lobby toward the check-in area, where he found the skinniest guy he'd ever seen manning the counter.

"I need a room," he muttered, pulling his wallet from the back pocket of his faded jeans.

"Single or double bed?"

"Double."

"Kitchenette?"

"I couldn't care less, kid." He pulled a wad of bills from his wallet and dropped them on the splintered oak counter.

"Okay then."

Ben scrawled a fake name and address on the clipboard handed to him then pushed it back at the clerk.

The guy barely gave him a second look before giving him a key and pointing to the elevator.

Two minutes later, Ben got off on the third floor and breathed in the scent of potpourri and lemon cleaner.

The hotel wasn't the type of accommodation he was used to, but for once he didn't care that the carpet beneath his black boots was frayed, or that the doors lining the narrow corridor were in desperate need of a fresh coat of paint. All he cared about was sleep. No telephones. No agents and managers and publicists. No reporters or photographers.

Just sleep.

He let himself into room 312. Didn't bother turning on the light, just let his gaze adjust to the darkness and zero in on the double bed in the center of the room. Within seconds, his boots were off, his leather jacket was tossed on the armchair, his jeans and boxers lay on the carpet, and his T-shirt somehow ended up caught in the ceiling fan.

Ben fell asleep before his head even hit the pillow.

Maggie found that her steps were unusually bouncy as she hurried down the street. Normally her feet killed after a shift at the Olive, especially on Friday nights, but the only part of her body that ached was the spot between her legs.

I'm going to have sex.

She didn't care if anyone thought she was pathetic. So what if her only source of sexual gratification was her infrequent trysts with Tony? She didn't have the time or energy for a relationship.

Relationships required effort—the only effort she had to make with Tony was unzipping his jeans.

Relationships drained you—with Tony, she was only drained after the first or second orgasm.

And Tony never made demands on her, never monopolized her time or made her feel that being a workaholic was something horrific. He worked as hard as she did, which officially made him the perfect man to get involved with.

Maggie dodged a rowdy group of teenagers loitering on the city sidewalk, and then waved at the hot dog vendor she passed every day on the way to work. Her apartment was only a few blocks from the bar, but she and Tony avoided going there. They always met in a hotel, where they could have fun all night long and then go their separate ways in the morning.

Another perk—not sharing an awkward breakfast together the morning after.

She reached the Lester Hotel a few minutes later, headed

straight for the counter, and said she wanted to check into room 312. The clerk, a very scrawny, very bored-looking young man, replied in a monotone that the room was already occupied.

"I know...he's expecting me," she said, her cheeks only warming slightly. She didn't care what this desk clerk thought of her. "There should be a spare key for me."

The guy turned around and stared at the dozens of keys hanging off the hooks on the wall, then plucked one with his long, bony fingers. As he handed her the key, she desperately wanted to offer to buy him a hot dog, or a cracker, anything to put some meat on those protruding bones.

Sex first, feed the check-in guy later.

Thanking the kid, she made her way to the elevator and rode the car up to the third floor. She and Tony had visited the Lester before, so she knew her way around and found the room quickly. Her breasts grew heavy as she stuck the key in the lock and turned it. God, she needed this. With her college exams coming up in a few weeks, not to mention the billiards tournament the bar was holding next month, she'd soon be up to her eyeballs in work.

If she wanted to play, tonight was it.

As she let herself into the room, she was instantly engulfed by shadows. She blinked and waited for her eyes to focus, while she tried to figure out the reason for the dead silence hanging over the room. No, wait, not dead silence. Her ears perked as the sound of light breathing floated from the direction of the bed.

"Oh, don't do this to me, Anthony," she chided softly, dropping her purse on the table beside her and turning to lock the door. "I see you three times a year, at least have the decency to stay awake."

No response.

A slow grin spread over her mouth as she took another step forward. She was tempted to flick on the lights and maybe stomp her foot to jar Tony from his slumber, but that wouldn't be fun, would it?

Instead, she reached for the hem of her black baby tee and pulled the shirt over her head. She unhooked her lacy bra, and it fell onto the carpet, followed by her short denim skirt, skimpy panties and the heels on her feet.

She shivered as the cool air met her naked skin, then she crept toward the edge of the bed, still grinning. Tony was about to get a hell of a wake-up call.

"C'mon, Tony," she murmured, "you only flew in from Nassau. Don't plead jet lag."

She was answered by a husky male groan.

"Ah, so he's alive," she teased, reaching for the corner of the flower-patterned blanket.

With a quiet chuckle, she slid under the covers and pressed her body against Tony's, fighting back a moan as his warm, rock-hard chest pressed against her bare breasts. Her nipples instantly hardened, the tight buds springing against the soft feathering of hair on that glorious chest.

She swung one leg over his muscular thighs, hoping the heat from her aching pussy might jumpstart his sluggish brain into action, but he remained motionless. The room was still bathed in darkness, and though she could barely see his face, it was obvious he was in a seriously deep sleep.

"I see how it is," she said, starting to grow annoyed. "Fine, you want me to raise you from the dead? How's this?"

She placed her hand directly on his crotch, a little surprised when she didn't find the cotton barrier of his briefs.

Since when did Tony sleep in the buff?

Not that she minded.

As a lazy heat began dancing through her veins, she dragged her index finger along the length of his shaft. Like his chest, it was rock-hard, and...bigger? No, it couldn't be.

She ran her finger over the tip of his cock, felt the drop of moisture there, and smiled as another groan broke through the silence. Finally. Signs of life.

His massive erection told her he'd be getting into the swing of things soon, and she was right. The second she squeezed his shaft, one powerful arm slid out and pulled her closer. She found herself crushed in his embrace, his cock still in her hand, while a pair of warm lips sought hers in the darkness.

His kiss stole the breath from her lungs and made her gasp against his hot mouth. There was nothing soft or gentle about it, just a greedy devouring, the hungry thrusts of his tongue, the sting of his teeth as he bit her lower lip.

Oh dear God, when did Tony start kissing like this?

And why hadn't he done it sooner?

The intensity of his kisses caused her to drop her hand from his throbbing erection, and all she could do was lose herself in the delicious sensations his mouth and tongue created in her body. Limbs turning to jelly. Moisture pooling between her legs. Nipples so tight it was almost painful.

A fire hotter than she'd ever experienced slowly swept over her. Crackling when he bit her lip again. Hissing when his hand cupped a breast.

And then he slid one finger into her sopping wet pussy and she was shocked to feel the ripples of an impending orgasm rising to the surface.

She clamped her teeth down on her bottom lip, trying to

stop herself from climaxing. It was too fast, too soon.

How is this possible? her overly-aroused brain demanded.

She'd slept with this guy dozens of times before, so why was her entire body swarming with unfamiliar—but totally incredible—sensations?

She pried open her eyelids, hoping if she let their gazes lock, she might make sense of it. She squinted, blinked as she searched his face in the dark, and then wondered why his features seemed more...rugged.

Her gaze drifted lower and settled on his arm—was that a tattoo? When had Tony gotten himself inked?

And why wasn't he tanned? He'd just come from the Bahamas, so really, he should have a—

"What's the matter, sweetheart?" came a sleepy voice.

The husky sound that filled the room made her sit up as if someone had shoved a ten-thousand-volt wire up her spine.

Why didn't she recognize his voice?

As a steady stream of panic rushed up her throat, she stared down at the dark head beside her, and repeated his question in her disorientated brain.

What was the matter?

In one very swift, very startling moment, Maggie knew exactly what the matter was.

She was in bed with a complete and total stranger.

Ben woke up with jolt, sucked out of his dream the way dust bunnies get sucked out from under the bed by a hungry vacuum cleaner. The shrill female yelp stung his ears, pleasure draining from his body like bathwater.

Christ, that dream. It even rivaled the one he'd had back in the ninth grade, where he'd fondled Cindy Mason's Double-D's. No Double-D's in this one, but a pair of delectable C's, and a female body with more curves than a lush valley. A hot mouth with an eager tongue. A tight wet pussy—

"Oh my God, I'm so sorry."

The mortified voice thrust Ben into a fully conscious state. As he quickly collected his bearings, he glanced over and saw that it was all real. There was a gorgeous redhead in bed with him, as naked as he was—and she looked horrified.

"What the fuck...?" He blinked a few times and finally forced his hand to reach for the lamp on the nightstand.

A pale yellow glow fell over the hotel room as he directed his gaze to the stranger next to him. She had green eyes, really nice green eyes, despite the fact that they flickered with deep alarm. Her cheeks were as red as her hair, and when he looked farther south, he saw that a crimson flush had spread over her very perky, very bare breasts.

The redhead caught him staring and let out another yelp, quickly pulling the bedcovers up to her chin to shield her nudity. Her domination of the blanket, however, left him fully exposed and a faint pang of embarrassment tugged at his gut when he noticed he still had the boner of all boners.

What the hell was going on here? He had no clue who this woman was, only that she was the sexiest sight he'd ever seen. Aside from those magnetic emerald eyes and knockout figure, she had high cheekbones, a dainty nose and a sensual mouth that was just a little bit crooked. He liked it, that small imperfection. It made her all the more...real.

He just wished she'd stop biting her bottom lip and wipe that deer-in-headlights expression off her flushed face.

"I'm so sorry," she said again as she edged toward the side of the bed, still clinging to the blanket. "I must be in the wrong

21

room."

He opened his mouth to answer, but for some inexplicable reason the power of speech completely eluded him. What the hell was he supposed to say anyway? No problem, thanks for giving me this stiffy?

As he watched her stumble off the bed in her blanket-toga, his confusion gave way to suspicion. Was she really in the wrong room? Sure, the skinny dude downstairs could have screwed up with the keys, but how likely was that? A much likelier possibility would be that this redhead was...damn it, was she *press*? Had she purposely snuck into his room and tried to seduce him in hopes of getting a juicy story to sell to the tabloids?

Oh shit.

Ben scrambled to cover himself with one of the flat pillows on the bed, then narrowed his eyes as the redhead scurried around the room, collecting items of clothing.

"Who are you?" he demanded in a tone that said he meant business.

She faltered for a moment, a black T-shirt clutched between her fingers. "What?"

"Are you a reporter?"

"Why would I be a reporter?" She appeared frazzled as she stared at the shirt in her hands and then shot him a pleading look. "Could you...could you just close your eyes for a minute while I get dressed?"

Oh, so *now* she was all prim and modest? She sure hadn't been that way when she was stroking his dick.

Deciding he was entitled to a little peek, he pretended to close his eyes while watching her through slitted eyelids. He got an out-of-focus glimpse of her scrambling to hook up her bra and his cock twitched with disappointment when her full breasts were finally covered. Would asking her to come back to bed be inappropriate?

Probably.

"Okay. I'm dressed."

Yes, she was. But the tight T-shirt and short denim skirt that did amazing things to her legs only confirmed she looked just as good clothed as she did naked.

"I'm mortified," she murmured. Then, looking as if she was offering a scrap of meat to a feral lion, she stepped forward and handed him the blanket.

He took the flowery material and draped it over himself as she continued to ramble on. "I was supposed to meet...a guy. He said this was his room number and I...I guess I got it wrong. I..." She began to stutter, "I don't usually break into strangers' hotel rooms, I promise. I just..." She finally drifted off, her cheeks growing redder by the second.

Strangers?

The word hung in the air, bringing with it another hefty dose of confusion. She didn't recognize him?

She actually *didn't* recognize him?

He wasn't conceited enough to think that all the women on the planet knew who he was, but his face had been splashed on every entertainment show in the country for weeks now. Even the elderly couple who did his dry-cleaning had heard of him, and they hadn't been to the movies since the fifties.

"I'm just going to leave now, okay?" she continued, jarring him from his thoughts. "I...I can't apologize enough for...*this*."

She swallowed, and then let out a flood of words that had him struggling to keep up. "I, uh...I work at a bar called the Olive Martini and it's near the corner of Broadway and 47th and if you're in the neighborhood, you can pop in and the drinks will be on the house." She sucked in a gust of air. "I know a free drink doesn't make up for...um, *this,* but it's all I can do."

She clamped her mouth shut and looked at him with wide, shameful eyes, as the humor of the situation finally settled in with full force. A complete stranger had just slipped into his bed, kissed the hell out of him, brought him to a level of hardness he'd never known, and now she was offering him free drinks to make up for it?

Laughter lodged in Ben's throat as he tried to formulate a sentence that might make the situation seem a little less absurd.

He never got the chance.

With an awkward smile and another look of terror, the redhead hurried for the door, just as a flash of pink from the carpet caught Ben's eye.

"Wait," he called as she reached for the door handle. "You forgot your—"

She slid out and closed the door with a soft click.

"—panties," he finished.

Chapter Two

Maggie tore down the street in a full-throttled run, sucking in the night air as if an overdose of oxygen would erase the pure humiliation sticking to her throat. She glanced over her shoulder, half expecting to see the sexy stranger she'd just mauled chasing after her. Nope. All she saw was the slow rush of people flowing out of one of the theaters, chattering about the show they'd just seen.

She knew her dark-haired hunk wasn't in the crowd because...hell, because lethal good looks like his would be impossible to miss.

How was it possible for someone to be that attractive?

Once he'd turned on the lights, she'd had to slam her mouth closed to avoid drooling all over the hotel room carpet. He had the kind of looks you only saw on Calvin Klein models these days—cobalt blue eyes, straight white teeth, dimples that melted your insides. But with a bit of an edge, which showed in the way his scruffy brown hair curled under his ears and in that tribal tattoo inked on his biceps. He had bad boy written all over him, which she found incredibly sexy, and all she knew was she'd better thank her lucky stars she'd gotten out of there.

Who knows what she would've done if she'd stayed even a second longer.

Probably fucked his brains out.

"Excuse me, coming through," Maggie called as she wove through the same group of teenagers she'd passed on the way to the hotel.

"Hey, baby, what's the rush?" one of the baggy-clothed kids asked with a laugh.

What's the rush? Um, maybe because she'd just stroked, caressed and made out with a complete stranger. If that didn't make a girl want to flee for the hills, what did?

She ignored the kids and pushed forward, her high heels clicking against the sidewalk. People kept getting in her way, slowing her down, when all she wanted was to get to her building and pretend she hadn't just committed the most reckless act of her twenty-five years.

Why hadn't Tony been there?

The question sliced through her so quickly that she stopped in her tracks. For the past five minutes she'd been beating herself over the head for winding up in a stranger's room, but there's no way she'd gotten the room number wrong. She'd written it on her hand, for God's sake!

Furrowing her brows, she flipped over her hand and stared at the three digits she'd scribbled on her palm. Yep. 312. The ink was starting to smear, but there was no mistaking the numbers. She'd gotten it right, which meant that Tony—that jerk—was to blame for this entire mess.

Why hadn't he shown up? He would've called her cell if the plan had changed, wouldn't he?

Maggie reached into her purse and rummaged around for her phone. She pulled it out, and then groaned. The battery was dead. She tried turning it on, but the thing simply wouldn't comply, so when she spotted an unoccupied payphone, she made a mad dash for it.

One quarter and five seconds later, she accessed her cell's

message service and heard Tony's voice.

"Hey, Mags, it's me. Listen, I've got some bad news. We had to make an emergency landing in Tallahassee. Some freak hurricane just swept in and the airline is delaying all the flights. I won't be able to get a flight out until tomorrow morning, but we're shit out of luck, babe. I have a meeting with a publisher in the afternoon and I'm heading out to Bora Bora at five. Looks like we'll see each other next time I'm in town. Probably the end of August. Say hi to the folks at the Olive for me."

Maggie hung up the phone and gritted her teeth. Say hi to the folks at the Olive for me?

Anger swirled in her stomach like a cluster of enraged butterflies, but deep down she knew she couldn't blame Tony for what had happened. He didn't control the weather or the airlines, and it wasn't his fault that a delay she hadn't known about had sent her into bed with another man.

Hell, she blamed herself for the embarrassment she felt. Why on earth hadn't she turned on the light when she walked in, instead of hopping into the bed and giving a stranger a hand job?

She was the moron, not Tony.

As her anger slowly dissolved, she took a few calming breaths. *It's not a big deal. Just a case of mistaken identity.*

It's not like she'd ever see her blue-eyed bad boy again, unless he decided to show up for that free drink she'd offered, but how likely was that? The man probably thought she was a nutcase.

A very astute assumption on his part.

Unable to stop it, a giggle tore out of her throat. It was a hysterical giggle, but she got some comfort from being able to laugh at the situation. The memory of her stranger's bewildered blue eyes as he lay on the bed with an impressive erection

27

flashed across her brain, turning the giggle into a full-out laugh. She'd never thought of herself as a wild woman, but after what she'd done tonight, she could never be accused of being *dull.*

Exiting the phone booth, Maggie resumed the walk home, her humiliation fading at each click of her heels. Okay, so she'd molested a man whose name she didn't even know. Big deal. He'd liked it. She'd liked it too. And they'd probably never cross paths again, so really, what harm had been done?

She held back another laugh and crossed the street, and by the time she reached the high-rise she called home, her nerves had started to calm.

She used her key to open the door to the lobby, and then stepped inside and greeted the security guard sitting behind the desk. Considering the building was only blocks away from Central Park, the rent should have been astronomical, but Maggie had lucked out. When she'd moved here from Queens, she'd thought she'd never be able to find a decent place that wouldn't drain her savings account, but on her very first day in the city she'd hit the jackpot.

Summer Windsor, a former waitress at the Olive, was subletting an apartment owned by her grandmother, and when Summer learned Maggie was currently living in a hotel, she'd offered her spare room. The rent was peanuts, which allowed Maggie to save for college, and she didn't even mind sleeping on the couch when Summer's grandmother came for a visit. In fact, she kind of looked forward to those visits. For a girl who'd grown up with zero family, sometimes it was nice having someone dote on her.

As she rode the elevator up to the tenth floor, she glanced at her watch. It was almost one a.m., which meant Summer was either sleeping, staying at her boyfriend's, or practicing her steel drum.

Please don't let it be option number three.

Her prayers went unanswered as she opened the door to the apartment and was instantly met by a wave of jingly notes, her roommate's rendition of "Under the Sea".

"You're still at it, huh?" Maggie called as she tossed her purse on the coffee table and collapsed on the couch.

"The wedding is in three days," Summer said from the other side of the room. "I have to practice."

Summer had set the drum up right in front of the small dining room window. More than once the people who lived in the building across from theirs screamed for her to keep her day job. It was almost comical, actually. Summer, the blonde-haired, blue-eyed accountant, banging away on a steel drum so that she could play it at a Jamaican wedding.

Summer had met Tygue Ortega, the man of her dreams, during a vacation to Montego Bay. The two had fallen head over heels for each other, and a month later Tygue moved to New York. The blonde and her dread-locked soulmate had been inseparable for more than a year now, and they were flying back to Jamaica in a few days to attend Tygue's brother's wedding.

Where Summer had gotten the idea to play the steel drum for the joyous event, however, totally eluded Maggie. She couldn't see Tygue asking his girlfriend to do it, which meant Summer had come up with that brainchild of an idea all on her own.

"I wasn't expecting you back tonight. Why aren't you with Tony?" Summer called, biting her lip in concentration as she banged away on the large instrument.

"You don't want to know," Maggie replied with a groan. She kicked off her heels and rested her legs on the glass coffee table.

Her ears got a much-needed reprieve as Summer stopped drumming. Her pale blue eyes flickering with curiosity, she rose from the stool and asked, "What happened?"

Summer walked over to the armchair next to the couch, and before her butt met the cushion, the entire story spilled out of Maggie's mouth. The words came out like an out-of-control freight train, starting from the moment she'd entered the hotel room to the way she'd scurried off like a dog with its tail between its legs.

By the time she finished, Summer was laughing uncontrollably, her expression a mixture of amazement, amusement and appreciation.

"Yes, laugh at me," Maggie said with a frown. "It makes me feel so much better."

"Oh God, I can't believe you did that," Summer blurted between giggles.

"Well, believe it. Honestly, I've never been more humiliated in my life. This even beat the time in fifth grade when that snotty Billy Turner made fun of me for being in foster care."

"Jeez, that *is* bad." Summer paused. "Was he hot, at least?"

"Hot is an understatement. He was..." She searched her vocabulary for the right adjective and came up empty-handed. "Indescribably good-looking."

Summer looked intrigued. "Nice bod?"

"Oh yeah." Maggie sighed. "And he had that whole rebel thing going on. Messy hair, tattoo on his left biceps, the I'm-too-cool-to-shave thing happening."

"Oooh, like Colin Farrell!"

"Who?"

"Your ignorance about sexy actors amazes me, Mags."

"This guy wasn't an actor. He was just a normal man trying

to get some sleep—until I showed up and nearly raped him."

"Did he like it?"

Maggie thought about the erection she'd stroked and fought back a shiver. "Oh yeah."

"Then no harm done." Summer shrugged. "He'll probably wake up tomorrow and think it was all a dream. He doesn't even know your name, unless you left your driver's license on the nightstand or something."

Maggie tucked a stray hair behind her ear and felt a warm flush spread over her face. "As a matter of fact, I did leave something behind."

Summer furrowed her eyebrows. "What?"

A wail slipped out of her mouth before she could stop it. "My underwear."

After a moment of silence, Summer burst out with a high-pitched giggle that had Maggie flinching.

"Priceless!" Summer cried, wiping tears of laughter from her pale eyelashes. "That is absolutely priceless!"

Her roommate's uncontrollable giggles brought back the wave of humiliation she'd tried to suppress. All she'd wanted to do tonight was, well, Tony. Instead, she'd made an idiot of herself in front of a complete stranger, and now had to live with the knowledge that she'd stripped naked, hopped into bed with a guy she didn't know and stuck her tongue down his throat.

She'd be sure to tell her children about it someday.

Not.

Ben strode down East 45th Street with a cup of coffee in his hand, breathing in the early morning air then grimacing when he inhaled a gust of car exhaust. As he paused in front of a jewelry store to take a sip of his coffee, he couldn't help but glance at his reflection in the large window.

What he saw was an unshaved jaw, circles under his eyes and a bloodshot expression, all of which confirmed what he already knew—he looked like shit.

It had been another sleepless night for him, only this time it had nothing to do with photographers lurking outside his house and everything to do with the redheaded tornado who had swirled into his room last night.

The more he replayed her stuttering explanation in his head, the less he believed his midnight visitor was one of the vultures. He believed it even less when he'd grabbed the morning paper at the kiosk across the street from the Lester and didn't see his picture on any of the tabloids on the rack.

If Red—as he now liked to call her—was a reporter, the story of her seduction would've at least made the *Tattler*, a rag known for keeping page space open for last-minute scoops.

Since it hadn't, he suspected she'd been telling the truth, that she'd ended up in the wrong room, in bed with the wrong guy.

And just like Cinderella, Red had left her prince a sweet little parting gift—a pair of pink lace panties.

And an offer for a free drink.

Under normal circumstances, Ben would have tossed the panties and passed on the booze, but last night had been anything but normal.

Sure, the make out session had been hot, but what turned him on most about her was that she genuinely hadn't known who he was.

Everything he did was highly publicized, from his appearances at the Oscars and the Golden Globes to his trysts with his fair share of models and starlets. Whether he wanted them to or not, women knew who he was. They gawked at him when he passed them on the street. They sent him thousands of fan letters, half of which had a nude photo or two tucked between scented stationery. He'd been called a heartthrob and a hunk, a devil and an angel, and the last time he'd appeared on *The Tonight Show* he'd almost gotten mobbed outside the studio.

So how in fiery hell didn't she know about him?

Ben had spent enough years tangled up in the film industry to know when somebody was bullshitting him, and he honestly didn't think he'd been lied to last night. Red had been oblivious to his celebrity status, and considering she hadn't salivated at the mere sight of him, he suspected she'd be unimpressed about it anyway.

Damn but that was a huge turn-on.

He quickened his pace, his gaze darting around in search of the lot where he'd left his car. He remembered it had been near that theater where he'd seen *Hamlet* last year, and there might have been a Starbucks around too, and a—

Strip club.

Ben stopped so abruptly he nearly fell over backwards. Oh man, oh man. All he'd wanted was to get the paparazzi off his back, but in retrospect, he really should've studied his surroundings before ditching his car. He'd parked in front of a damn strip joint.

So much for avoiding scandals.

Resisting the urge to hit himself over his own stupidity, Ben was startled when he noticed a crowd beginning to gather at the curb. He moved closer, growing more and more uneasy as he spotted an army of police officers and yards of yellow crime-scene tape.

Surrounding his shiny silver Lexus.

What the fuck?

Taking a step back, Ben tried to blend into the crowd. The Lexus, he noticed when he peeked over a woman's head, was stripped completely. The doors were gone, the engine too, from the looks of it, and it looked like a pack of hyenas had pounced on it sometime during the night and picked it clean. That didn't surprise him. What *did* was the presence of New York City's finest.

Why did the cops care about his car?

Ben found out soon enough as the woman in front of him leaned over and whispered something to her friend.

"It's Ben Barrett's car," she hissed.

Her friend, a chubby blonde, let out a gasp. "The movie star?"

"Yep. I heard one of the officers mention it." The woman lowered her voice to a breathy whisper. "They think he's been abducted."

What?

It took every ounce of willpower to keep his jaw off the dirty sidewalk.

Head spinning, Ben edged away from the murmuring crowd and walked as casually as his legs would allow. He reached into his back pocket for his cell phone but found nothing. Damn, his cell had been in the car. He glanced around, noticed the coffee shop at the corner, and made a beeline for it.

He knew he had to call his agent and clear up this whole ridiculous mess, a plan that became vital the second he entered the café and heard his name blaring from the television screen over the counter.

"Bad-boy action star Ben Barrett is believed to have been

abducted," a nasal-voiced reporter was saying into her microphone. "His car was found stripped and abandoned in front of a local New York City club, and police fear the worst."

Shoving the rim of his cap as low as it would go, Ben paused in front of the long chrome counter and glanced at the screen. He instantly swallowed a groan when he noticed that the female reporter was reciting her broadcast from the sidewalk directly in front of the Lester Hotel.

He bit back a curse when the skinny desk clerk entered the frame.

"I'm now talking to Derek Dorsey, an employee of the hotel where Ben Barrett was last seen. Derek, what can you tell us about your encounter with Barrett?"

Ben curled his hands into fists.

"Well, he looked very agitated," the kid said, his eyes darting from the microphone to the camera trained on him. "He looked nervous too."

"And what do you mean by nervous?"

"I think he was on drugs."

The reporter feigned shock. "How tragic!"

"And he wasn't alone," the kid added, then waved at the camera and mouthed, "Hi, Mom."

"Are you saying Ben Barrett met someone here last night?"

"Not someone. A *woman*. She came in an hour after he did and requested the key to his room." Dorsey grinned, which caused his bony face to jut out awkwardly. "I think they were engaging in sexual relations, Bette."

The blood rushing to his head prevented Ben from hearing the end of the interview. Fists clenched, he stalked across the deserted café and headed for the payphone in the narrow corridor leading to the restrooms.

He punched the number for the operator and made a collect call to his agent.

"Ben, are you okay?" Stu Steinberg's voice boomed after they'd been connected.

"I'm fine," Ben said with a sigh. He rubbed the stubble dotting his chin. "What the hell is going on?"

"You're asking me?" Stu shot out a string of four-letter words. "Why was your car found gutted in front of a strip joint?"

"I was trying to lose the press. Then I checked into a hotel to get some sleep." Even to his own ears the answer sounded feeble at best and preposterous at worst.

"And who's this hooker you were with last night?"

Ben's features hardened. "I wasn't with a hooker, Stu. You know that's not my style."

His agent's voice mocked him from the other end of the line. "You want to know what I *do* know about you, Ben? You're a fucking idiot. You just inherited ten million bucks from a woman you had no business sleeping with—"

"Gretchen and I never—"

"So I told you to lay low, but did you listen? Oh no, you went out and caused a media storm. Do you realize how many calls I've gotten from the press this morning? Not to mention the police."

"Stu—"

"They think you were abducted by a crazed whore, for Christ's sake!"

"Stu—"

"Here's what we're going to do, Ben. I'll call Mary and have her fly to New York. She'll sit down with you and figure out a way to spin this so that you don't look like a complete jerk. But first we need to call off the cops and tell them Mr. Movie Star is alive and well. *Capiche?*"

"You're not Italian, Stu, but yes, that sounds good. As for Mary, tell her to stay in LA. There's nothing to spin here."

"Are you insane?"

Ben gripped the receiver so tightly he feared it might shatter into a million little pieces. "I'm not insane. I'm just tired. I'm tired of being hounded and harassed and I haven't slept in a week, Stu. So go ahead and tell the police to call off their investigation, but don't expect me to make a solitary public appearance to explain this ridiculous story the press has yet again concocted." .

"So what, you're just going to fuel the fire by disappearing off the face of the earth?" Stu demanded, sounding angrier than ever.

"That's exactly what I'm going to do. I'm going to disappear, Stu. You wanted me to lay low, well, I'll lay low. I'm not answering any calls, I'm not meeting with Mary or anyone from the PR firm. In fact, I'm not doing a fucking thing."

"What's that supposed to mean?"

"It means Ben Barrett is officially out of the limelight. For how long, I don't know. But I'm done, Stu. If I don't get some peace and quiet I'll end up in a nuthouse, so placate the cops, say whatever you want to the reporters and leave me the hell alone. *Capiche?*"

"Bye, Maggie!"

Maggie smiled at the two little girls standing in the doorway before signing out at the community center where she volunteered. She waved at the counselor who doubled as a receptionist, gave each of the giggling girls by the door a big hug good-bye and stepped through the double doors leading outside.

Finally alone, she let out the weary sigh that had been lodged in her chest all afternoon.

Considering she'd gotten a grand total of three hours sleep last night, she probably should've skipped volunteering and stayed in bed, but as usual, her sometimes-irritating sense of responsibility prevented her from being lazy.

Her work at the Joshua Broger Community Center was too important, and she knew the kids were always disappointed when she didn't show up—which was rare. Most of the children who came to the center lived in foster homes, and having been a part of the foster system for thirteen years of her life, Maggie only wished she'd had a place like the Broger Center to visit. Somewhere to get help with her homework, or talk to a counselor, or just spend some time with other children her age.

Volunteering, she felt like she was making a difference. And she was. She knew that.

But she also wished she could make a difference and get paid for it at the same time.

The bottom line—she was tired. Exhausted. No, so past exhausted she felt like an extra from a zombie movie.

It certainly didn't help that instead of getting her quick Tony fix, she'd just ended up more frustrated than she'd been to begin with.

She'd considered taking that vibrator Summer had given her out of its unopened box, but somehow the idea of turning to a plastic male organ wasn't too appealing. Not when she'd been so close to having the real thing.

With a stranger.

Right. Who could forget that?

Who could forget *him*? a little voice teased.

Definitely not her. Oh no, instead of banishing the embarrassing memories from her mind, Maggie had stayed up half the night thinking about her mysterious bad boy. If she were a braver woman, she might have stuck around and coyly suggested they enjoy a few rounds of anonymous sex. At least then she wouldn't have spent the night lying in bed, frustrated and aching for release.

Sighing again, Maggie approached the curb and focused on flagging down a taxi and leaving Harlem.

She found a cab fairly quickly, though the drive across town wasn't as quick. She was two minutes late when the taxi driver maneuvered out of lane-to-lane Saturday evening traffic and finally crept to a stop in front of the Olive. She handed the man a couple of bills, then hurried inside and made her way across the bar toward the doors leading to the employees' lounge.

"Hey, Trish," she called to the brunette behind the counter.

The second she saw her, Trisha dropped the receipts in her hands and dashed over. "Maggie, walk faster," she hissed.

As Trisha grabbed her arm and practically dragged her through the back corridor, Maggie looked at her with wide eyes. "What's the matter?"

"Just move."

Trisha pushed open the door to the lounge, staying on Maggie's heels as she headed for the small bank of lockers at the far end of the room. Spinning the combination lock, Maggie pulled open the locker and shot her co-worker a sideways glance.

"Well?"

Trisha shifted from one foot to the other, her dark eyes

dancing. "I think Ben Barrett is here."

Maggie slipped out of her jeans and changed into the denim skirt the waitresses were forced to wear. "Who?"

"Who? *Who?* I can't believe you just asked me that." Trisha began to speak in a patient voice reserved for small children and rabid dogs. "*Heart of a Hero? McLeod's Revenge? The Warrior?*"

She blinked. "What, he writes romance novels or something?"

Trisha let out a shriek. "No, you idiot. Those are movies he's starred in. You're honestly telling me you don't know who Ben Barrett is?"

Maggie shrugged, then pulled her T-shirt over her head and exchanged it for a V-neck black tank. Kicking off her sneakers, she strapped a pair of black heels on her feet and turned back to the enraged brunette.

"Trish, the last time I went to the movies, I was ten. My foster parents took all the kids to see a Disney movie." She poked her tongue in her cheek. "Come to think of it, that's the *only* time I've gone to the movies."

"What about television?" Trisha asked with a frustrated tilt of her chin. "You've got to watch television."

"Not really." Maggie paused. "If I'm not too tired, I watch cooking shows with Summer. She's been trying to learn about Jamaican cuisine so she can cook for Tygue. The first time she tried we all got food poisoning, so—"

"Forget it," Trisha cut in, not looking amused. "All I'm going to say is I think a movie star is sitting in the booth near the pool table."

Maggie didn't really care, but she felt she owed it to her friend to ask, "What makes you think that?"

"Well, he came in about an hour ago, walked up to the bar and ordered a glass of sparkling water. He gave Matt a hundred-dollar bill and said he wanted to be left alone."

"Gee, then it *must* be him."

Trisha ignored her. "He's wearing a baseball cap and hiding behind a newspaper, but he looks *sooo* familiar. I walked past him a few times and I swear it's him. And there's more."

"I can't wait to hear it."

"I saw on the news earlier that the police found Ben Barrett's car abandoned a few blocks from here."

"Hmmm. Maybe he couldn't find parking out front."

"*Then,*" Trisha continued, still ignoring her, "the cops gave a statement saying that Ben Barrett is alive and well, just a victim of some NYC car vandalism. I think the whole thing was a scam, and that he ditched his car because he's on the run."

Maggie's head began to spin. "Why do you think I'm interested in any of this, Trish?"

"Because I need you to find out if it's him or not!" Trisha wailed.

"How would I know? I have no clue what the guy looks like, remember?"

"Well, *I* can't do it. I've already walked by his booth too many times. If I do it again it'll raise his suspicions and he'll take off."

Maggie rolled her eyes. She knew Trisha was bored shitless with her boyfriend, and that sometimes her predicament caused her to poke her nose into other people's business.

But this was just ridiculous.

As the two women left the lounge, Trisha continued to push. "So will you find out if it's him?"

"Nope. Ask Matt."

"I did, he told me to leave the poor man alone."

"I second that notion." She stopped by the counter and reached over it to retrieve an apron. Then she grinned at the bartender. "So, Booth Five slipped you a hundred, huh?"

"Yep. And I suppose Trish told you she thinks he's a big star in disguise?" Matthew shot the other waitress an annoyed look before growing serious. "Look, he said he doesn't want to be bothered, which is why I've been keeping *this one*—" Matt hooked a thumb at Trisha, "—away from the poor guy."

Trisha glowered at him. "If you'd just let me go over there, I promise not to bug him."

"Yeah right," he hooted.

Linda White, the evening manager, walked up with a frown on her face, and the good-natured bantering came to a halt. Linda wasn't strict by any means, but her conservative nature and lack of humor turned off most of the staff.

No matter how grumpy she could be, Maggie still liked the older woman and greeted her with a smile. "Hey, Linda."

The manager ignored the greeting. "Guys, I've been here for an hour and not once has someone gone over to Booth Five to refill the customer's drink."

Looking sheepish, Matt opened his mouth to reply but Linda silenced him by holding up her hand. "You know I have no problem with the casual atmosphere we've created here, but we're going to need to change a few habits and start acting in a more professional manner. Jeremy will be in New York next week, checking out his investment, so it's time to shape up, all right?"

Jeremy Henderson was the sole owner of the bar, but as far as Maggie knew, the man had only stepped foot in the place half a dozen times since the grand opening. He left the actual running of the bar to managers like Linda, and the only sign that Henderson actually owned the Olive was his autograph on Maggie's paychecks.

She could see, though, why the owner's sudden decision to pop in would unnerve Linda, who'd pretty much singled-handedly run the Olive for six years now.

"No problem," Maggie said, in response to Linda's order to shape up. She tied her pinstriped apron around her waist and reached for her order pad. "I'll check on Booth Five and see how he's doing."

As Maggie headed for the booth, she could feel Trisha's eyes boring into her back. She'd seen that flicker of irritation on her friend's face, but too bad. Considering Linda had just given them a speech about professionalism, Maggie didn't think letting Trisha approach the *movie star* would achieve that.

Like Trisha said, the mysterious stranger had his face hidden behind a newspaper, which really wasn't all that suspicious when you thought about it. People read newspapers every day. People read newspapers in bars every day. It didn't mean they were celebrities.

"Sorry to disturb you, sir, but would you like some more water?" she said to the Sports section.

There was no response from the man behind the paper. Fighting back irritation, she added, "Or maybe you'd like something else. A beer?"

Very slowly, the newspaper lowered.

A second later, Maggie's gaze collided with a pair of familiar blue eyes.

"Hello again," her stranger said pleasantly, the corner of his mouth lifting in a small grin.

"Oh," she squeaked.

Chapter Three

Oh? *Oh?* Couldn't she have thought of anything better to say to the man she'd hopped into bed with last night?

She tried to look casual despite the incessant thumping of her heart. God, she hadn't thought she'd see him again. Yet here he was.

And either she was crazy, or she hadn't paid close enough attention yesterday, but he seemed to have gotten even better looking. Had to be the clothes. Naked, he'd had sex written all over him, but now, in that leather jacket and faded blue jeans, he looked sexy and dangerous and completely edible.

As if the hotel-room disaster had happened seconds ago rather than hours, Maggie's embarrassment returned with full-force, slithered up her spine and settled in the back of her throat. Along with it, though, came a spark of arousal at the memory of how incredible this guy's mouth had felt on hers. How warm his hands had been when they'd gripped her waist, and how hard his—

"No need to look so terrified," he quipped, running a hand through his dark hair. "I won't bite, you know."

Yes, you will. You already did, she wanted to add, thinking of the way his teeth had nibbled on her bottom lip.

"Um, I didn't think we'd see each other again." She lowered her voice so that nobody could overhear. "I guess you're here for that free drink."

"Actually, no." The other side of his mouth lifted so that a full-blown grin played on his lips. "I'm here to return something."

"Return—oh!" She gulped.

"I know how attached women can be to their panties. Apparently it's like losing a limb."

Was she blushing? Oh yes, she most certainly had to be blushing.

"I..."

She would've finished her sentence if not for the sharp fingernail that poked the small of her back. The French-manicured perpetrator was obviously Trisha, who gave a strangled cough that sounded like "ask him" before she scurried away. Knowing Trisha would probably bug her all night if she didn't interrogate the guy, Maggie decided to humor her friend.

Besides, the chances of her winding up in the arms of a supposed movie star were slim to none, so she was fairly confident betting against Trisha's farfetched suspicion.

Still feeling the blush imprinted on her cheeks, she lowered her voice and asked, "This is going to sound absolutely ridiculous but is your name Ben Barrett?"

His grin faded as if a switch had gone off. "Why do you ask?"

She shrugged. "One of the waitresses here just thinks you're, well, this guy named Ben Barrett."

He didn't answer.

"He's an actor or something," she added.

Still no answer. Wonderful. Had she just insulted him? Maybe he was one of those celebrity look-alikes who was constantly hassled on the streets and got pissed off whenever somebody pointed out the resemblance.

Opening her mouth to apologize for pressing him, she was surprised when he met her gaze and said, "Yes."

"Yes what?"

"I'm Ben Barrett."

The apology died on her lips. *What?*

"The actor," he added with a faint smile.

All she could do was stare. He had to be kidding, of course.

Are you a reporter?

His question from the night before floated into the forefront of her brain, bringing with it a niggling sense of doubt. Why had he asked that? Because, really, only a man who was used to having reporters around him would ask if she was one.

Which meant...

Oh God, could he actually be *not* kidding?

She focused her gaze on his gorgeous face. "Is this a joke?"

His features grew pained. "No."

"You're really this Ben Barrett guy?"

"Lower your voice, Red, will ya?"

Red?

"My name's Maggie," she said, absently playing with the hem of her apron. "And I don't get it. Why don't you want anyone to know who you are?"

"I..." He rubbed his temples. "I don't want to be bothered. I've had a bitch of a time lately, with reporters hounding me. I just want to be left alone."

She raised her eyebrows. "So you decided to come to one of the busiest bars in Manhattan on the busiest night of the weekend?"

"I wanted to see you."

Her heart skipped a beat and then went into a galloping frenzy as his words settled in and warmed various parts of her body. He'd wanted to see her? A complete stranger who'd violated his bed?

He's a guy, Maggie.

Right. Movie star or not, he probably hadn't been too outraged at being violated.

"You don't even know me," she found herself squeaking.

"Well, that can be easily changed," he replied, the grin returning to his rugged face.

He said it in a voice so smooth with confidence and so heady with sexual promise, her body grew even warmer in response. No, not warm. Hot. Burning hot.

Hoping he couldn't see her nipples poking against her shirt, she swallowed, desperate to allow some moisture back into her mouth. "I'm working."

I'm working? Again, that's all she could come up with? What about, *Look, you're hot but I don't have time for complications right now.*

And she was pretty sure Ben would be just that—a complication. He might be sexy as sin, and yeah, his voice gave her shivers that were completely foreign to her, but there was no doubt in her mind that he was trouble.

She didn't have time to play games with a movie star, no matter how delicious he looked. That's why she preferred guys like Tony. Tony didn't have time for games, or much of anything, for that matter. With him, it was simply *let's have some hot sex and see you later.*

"I'm fully aware that you're working," he said, his voice snapping her attention back to the present. "I've also waited tables myself before, so I'm pretty sure you'll have a break in a couple hours, right?"

She nodded. "Nine o'clock." Damn, why had she said that?

He returned the nod. "Good. So we'll talk then."

"We will?"

"Yep."

Maggie gulped, her insides swirling with both anticipation and indignation. How arrogant was this guy? He just assumed she'd spend her dinner break hanging out with him? Like she had no other options? Like his sex appeal was so strong she just couldn't wait to be alone with him and—

"I'll meet you out front at nine," she blurted.

Then she headed back to the counter and tried to convince herself that the only reason she'd agreed to meet him was to get some answers and that his good looks and sexy voice had absolutely no effect on her.

Ben smothered a laugh as he watched Maggie scurry away. He wondered if she realized her tendency to blush pretty much eliminated any chance of covering up her emotions. He'd only been around her twice, but Ben was able to pick up on everything she was feeling from that telltale blush on her cheeks.

Crimson red meant she was embarrassed. He'd seen it last night, and again today, when he'd brought up the subject of her panties.

Scarlet red meant she was angry, which had been evident when he'd announced they'd be meeting up during her break.

And rosy pink...well, that was a clear and undeniable shade of her arousal.

She was attracted to him. He knew it, and he was pretty sure she knew it too. Hell, it would be damn hard to deny it, seeing as the sexual tension had hissed like a rattlesnake the second their eyes met.

He took a sip of water and reached for the novel he'd tucked into the pocket of his leather jacket. Nine o'clock, she'd said. Left him with a few hours to kill, but that's why he'd bought the book. He'd tried reading it earlier, when he'd sat in Central Park, but he'd been too tense and too alert. Losing yourself in a paperback thriller was hard when you were constantly glancing over your shoulder, waiting for someone to ask for an autograph, or for a photographer to pop out from the other side of the bike path and snap your picture.

Maybe that's why he'd come here tonight. He knew sooner or later he'd have to figure out where to spend the night, but calling up the few acquaintances he knew in the city or attempting to check into another hotel appealed to him as much as having his back waxed.

Why should he risk it anyway? His so-called friends would sell him out in a nanosecond, and if the other hotel clerks in Manhattan were anything like the guy from the Lester, Ben would only find himself on the news again.

He'd thought about renting a car and driving upstate, maybe checking into a little B & B, but something had stopped him from leaving the city.

No, not something. Someone.

More specifically, the curvaceous redhead whose green eyes kept darting in his direction.

Damn, but she looked even sexier now that he was fully awake. All that silky red hair that couldn't decide if it wanted to be wavy or straight. Those emerald eyes. The tight little body. Looking at her now, he kinda wished he'd asked her to stay in his hotel room last night. Would've been a lot more fun than the self-gratification session he'd had to indulge in after she'd left him with a raging hard-on.

Though he couldn't really explain it, this woman had been on his mind from the second he'd opened his eyes this morning to the moment she'd walked up to his booth, and now he was glad he'd listened to the strange urge that told him to see her. He'd been on edge all day, but sitting here in this booth with nothing to do but read a book and wait for Maggie to go on break, he didn't feel as stiff. The tension in his back had eased, his muscles were relaxed, and for the first time in a long time he was relishing in the feeling of being anonymous.

From the corner of his eye, he saw Maggie exchange a few words with that brown-haired waitress who'd been eyeing him all evening. The sight of the two women whispering caused a sliver of unease to pierce through him. Damn. Were they talking about him?

Was Maggie, at the moment, confirming his identity or denying it?

The latter became likelier, as Maggie's fellow waitress frowned, then pouted, then glanced over at Ben with supreme disappointment.

He stuck his nose in his book to hide a smile. Why had she covered for him? She really had no reason to do that, but the fact that she'd respected his request for privacy pleased him to no end.

When she sidled past his booth again, he couldn't help but shoot her a grateful smile. She didn't smile back, just spared a brief look in his direction and sauntered by.

Was that annoyance he just saw flickering in her emerald gaze?

Ben turned around and watched as Maggie maneuvered her way around the large, dimly-lit room, which slowly beginning to fill up. Most of the scattered tables and wall-to-wall booths were occupied, and a popular hip-hop song now blared from the bar's speaker system. Since it was Saturday night, Ben knew the place would soon be filled to capacity, but he couldn't bring himself to duck out just yet.

He was far too fascinated with the redhead across the room.

Her ass looked tempting in that short denim skirt, making Ben's hand tingle with the urge to squeeze that sexy feminine curve. His gaze drifted north, to her slim back and all that wavy red hair cascading down it, and he was startled to find his dick hardening at the sight.

Jeez. When was the last time he'd gotten an erection from ogling a woman's back?

Lowering his eyes to the novel, he tried to shake off the desire raging through his blood, but though he managed to get a fair amount of reading done, Maggie's presence constantly distracted him.

His senses kicked into overdrive, trying to remember every detail from last night. How sweet her hair had smelled when it brushed against his cheek. The heat of her body pressed against his. The taste of her lips. The urgency of her tongue. The way her pussy had tightened over his finger when he'd slid it inside her.

The mouth-watering memories only made it more difficult to keep his cock in check. Finally, unable to concentrate on the thriller in front of him, he closed the book and glanced at his watch again. Quarter to nine. Man, time sure flew by when you were fantasizing about a hot redhead while pretending to read.

"Do you think it's him?" came a high-pitched female voice.

Shit. Even in his fairly isolated booth, Ben knew the two women sitting on the tall stools by the counter had a clear view of him. He yanked on his baseball cap at the same time he heard the two words that made him cringe—"Ben Barrett."

All the muscles that had relaxed stiffened again, and his brain ordered him to get out before either of the females at the bar decided to approach him.

Maggie's throaty voice stopped him from rising.

"Sorry, honey, it's not who you think it is." She gave a loud, exaggerated sigh that made Ben's lips twitch. "I thought it was him too, but it's not. I already asked."

"That sucks," said one of the women. "I heard he's in the city."

"If he is, he wouldn't come to a place like this." From his vantage point, Ben noticed that the smile on Maggie's lips seemed forced. "Big celebrities like that rent suites at the Plaza and entertain high-class call girls."

Ben choked back a laugh. He was tempted to march over there and kiss her senseless for the way she'd covered for him— *again.* Instead, he waited patiently for another fifteen minutes, then stood up when he heard Maggie tell the blond-haired bartender she'd be back in thirty.

Tucking his book in his pocket, he hopped out of the booth and headed for the door. He breathed in the late evening air. A few moments later, Maggie walked out of the bar. She paused near the streetlight by the curb, the pale yellow light causing her hair to appear redder and brighter. Like a halo of fire kindled by the calm evening breeze.

"Hey," he greeted her with a smile.

She, on the other hand, stared him down with obvious wariness in her eyes. And there it was again, that annoyance. What the hell was up with that?

"Hi." She held on to the thick strap of her oversized purse. "I have a half hour for my dinner break. I usually grab a hot dog."

"Let's go," he said easily.

She nodded and then pushed forward, her high heels clacking against the pavement.

Ben fell into step with her and cocked his head. "You look angry."

She shot him a sideways glance. "What makes you think that?"

He shrugged. "Well, are you?"

"A little."

"Because I showed up at your place of work?"

Her hands dropped to her hips as she stopped walking. "Yes. Thanks to you, I've spent the last three hours as your bodyguard, trying to keep every female in the place away from you."

He had to grin. "I never asked you to do that."

"You didn't have to. You turned white as mayo when I asked who you were, it was obvious you didn't want to be bothered." She paused. "Besides, I owe you. Celebrity or not, I still barged into your room last night."

With a frown, she resumed walking. He quickened his pace to keep up with her, oddly pleased that his celebrity status was an obvious thorn in her side.

It sure as hell was a thorn in his.

"So what do you want?"

She got right to the point, which he suspected she did a lot. Just another item to add to his already growing list of reasons why he liked her.

"I told you, I came to return something."

They stopped in front of a hot dog vendor, who Maggie

greeted by name. She ordered a dog with all the fixings, paid the man, and turned back to Ben.

"So that's it? You came by only to return my underwear?"

A loud cough sounded. Glancing over, Ben saw the hot dog vendor raising his bushy eyebrows at them.

Maggie waved a dismissive hand. "Just a figure of speech, Joe. Pretend you didn't hear that."

She said good-bye and gestured for Ben to follow her. Moments later they were leaning against a brick wall a few yards away, and Ben couldn't help but be impressed as he watched Maggie eat.

It had been a while since he'd met a woman who dined in anything less than a five-star restaurant, and if he'd even dared to suggest to a date they indulge in some street meat he'd probably get slapped. But Maggie, she looked completely comfortable as she chewed on her hot dog and wiped ketchup from the corner of her delectable mouth.

She didn't seem to notice the people hurrying by or the sound of cars whizzing down Broadway, and when a cop car sped past, sirens blazing, she didn't even blink. She acted like having dinner in the middle of a busy street was no big deal.

"Is there a reason why you're staring at me like that?" she asked, jarring him from his thoughts.

He shrugged. "I like the way you eat."

One reddish-brown eyebrow lifted. "Is that some weird pick-up line?"

A laugh slipped from his throat. Damn, he liked her. "No, just an honest-to-God compliment. It's been a while since I've met a woman who eats something other than salad."

Maggie made a face as she swallowed back the last bite of her hot dog. "If my meals consisted of salad, I'd die of malnutrition." She wiped her mouth demurely with a napkin and then tossed it in a nearby trashcan. "Now, listen up, Mr. Movie Star."

He couldn't help but grin. "I'm all ears."

"What do you want from me?" Her hands dropped to her hips again, and he noticed her fingernails were short and unpolished. "I already apologized for last night and you passed on my offer for a free drink, so why are you here?"

Before he could answer, she narrowed those emerald eyes. "You're not going to sue me, are you?"

Taken aback, he said, "What?"

"Sue me. For sexual harassment or something."

"Of course I'm not going to sue you."

"You better not." She scowled at him. "It would never hold up in court, anyway."

He stared at her, bewildered. Who was this woman? One minute she was angry with him, the next she was accusing him of launching a lawsuit. It was exasperating, but in a cute way, and as he stood there looking at her, he finally figured out what it was that drew him to her.

It wasn't the fact that she was oblivious to his career, or the way her curvy body had felt pressed against his. It wasn't the appealing blushing, or the killer legs, or how great her ass looked in that short skirt.

He liked her because she treated him like a...human being.

She knew who he was now, and she still didn't care. She wasn't trying to impress him, wasn't holding her tongue because he was a big, bad movie star. Aside from his mother, this redheaded waitress was the first female who wasn't scared to tell him exactly what she was thinking.

"Okay, then what do you want?" she repeated, her lips

pursed in what looked like annoyance. "And don't say a date, because I really don't have time for that."

He laughed again and decided this was the best conversation he'd ever had with a woman.

"What do I want," he repeated thoughtfully. He pulled one hand out of his pocket and with it came those pink panties. With a chivalrous bow, he handed her the silky wad. "First, to return these. I don't want your pretty little butt getting cold."

A whisper of a smile crossed her luscious mouth as she tucked the underwear into her purse. "My butt is just fine, Mr. Barrett. I do own more than one pair of panties. And second?"

"Second?"

"You said the underwear was first. What's second?"

He poked his tongue in his cheek and eyed her, experiencing one of those rare times when words escaped him. What did he want? Well, he knew what he *needed*, and that was to figure out where to spend the night without ending up on the news again.

What he *wanted*, though, was nothing more than to pull this quirky redhead into his arms and kiss the hell out of her. And then maybe go back to her place and *fuck* the hell out of her.

Then again...who said that his needs and wants were mutually exclusive?

He needed a bed.

He wanted this woman in bed with him.

Why couldn't he have both?

"You're doing it again," Maggie blurted out, jolting him back to reality.

"Doing what?"

"Staring at me. Be honest, do I have something stuck

between my teeth?"

He laughed. "No."

Her features grew taut again. "Okay then, we've wasted enough time here, Mr. Barrett. I have to go back to work and you—"

"Let me stay at your place tonight."

Maggie slammed her jaw closed so abruptly she could hear a few teeth rattling around in her mouth. Was this man insane?

Let me stay at your place tonight.

Seven words she'd never expected to hear, and yet the second he'd uttered them, a thrill shot up her spine.

Fine, so maybe the idea of ditching Summer and her steel drum and bringing this sex god into her domestic space was seriously tempting. But unlike most people, Maggie was pretty skilled at resisting temptation.

Yeah, Eve probably that thought too, before she took a chunk out of that apple.

Maggie stared into Ben's dark blue eyes and wondered if he was joking. He didn't look like it. No amusement in that sexy gaze. No I'm-just-kidding-around-with-you expression.

Did he actually think she would let him stay at her apartment?

"No offense or anything, but are you strapped for cash?" she asked with just a tad of hesitance in her tone. The guy's financial status wasn't any of her business, but she had to know.

"No, I'm doing all right in the finance department."

He took a step back, but she still felt the heat radiating from his lean body. The leather jacket he wore didn't emphasize his muscled arms or rippled chest, but she remembered those details well. She wondered if he had any other tattoos she might have missed in the dark. Then she wondered why her thighs trembled at the idea there might be more.

For God's sake, stop checking him out and focus.

Right. It didn't matter how many tattoos he might have hidden on that hard body of his. That was no reason to invite him to stay with her.

"Okay, so you've got money," she said, crossing her arms over her chest. "Which means you can afford to check into a hotel."

"I'd much rather stay with you, Red."

Eyes narrowed, she asked, "Are you in trouble with the law?"

"No. I just need a place to stay."

"Why?"

"Do you always ask so many questions?" he teased.

"When a stranger asks to crash at my place, yes."

"We're not strangers." He moved closer again and dipped his head so they were at eye level. "We've been in bed together, remember?"

He had to bring that up again, didn't he?

"I just don't get why you're asking me this."

He sighed, and his warm breath tickled the bridge of her nose. "Here's the short version, Red. As you now know, I'm somewhat of a celebrity. I haven't slept in days because the press is on my back for a silly scandal they fabricated. This morning they thought I was abducted. The cops gave a statement that I wasn't, but the media is still camped out in front of my house."

"No friends you could call?"

"Friends?" He made a bitter noise that sounded like a cross between a laugh and a snort. "Let me enlighten you about my so-called friends. A guy I grew up with, inseparable since we were six years old, I was best man at his wedding. Last year he sold pictures he had of me from his bachelor party for a cool quarter million. Sound like a friend to you?"

Maggie swallowed. "Ouch." Then, realizing she'd let her sympathy distract her, she said, "Okay, so you've succeeded in making me feel sorry for you."

"I don't expect you to feel sorry—"

"But it doesn't mean you can coax a free bed out of me."

He took a step closer and lowered his head so that his lips brushed her ear. "I doubt you need much coaxing, Red. It's obvious you want me in your bed as much as I want to be there."

"Excuse me?" A spark of anger lit in her stomach at the sheer arrogance dripping from his tone. "Where do you get off?"

A lazy grin spread across his mouth. "Well, last night, I got off while lying in bed thinking about a certain redhead who'd started fondling me."

Heat rolled through her like an avalanche. Had he just said what she thought he did?

"Tonight, though," he added with that wicked grin of his, "I figured maybe we'd get off together."

The arrogance returned to his tone, and her arousal was replaced with another flicker of anger. Guys were never this forward with her, and though his flirting was kind of cute, the way he assumed he could just snap his fingers and get her into bed was almost insulting.

"Look, I get it. You apparently think you're God's gift to women. But let me tell you something, Ben Barrett, I'm not one of those girls who rips off her shirt in the presence of a big celebrity, okay? In fact, the last thing I want to do is get involved with someone like—"

He kissed her.

Just like that. No permission, no warning, he just slammed his hot mouth on hers and kissed her.

If any other man had cut her off like that she would've probably slugged him, but Maggie found herself unable to move under the assault of Ben's lips. Her bones seemed to melt, her limbs flopped around like a wad of Play-Doh being pulled in all directions by the hands of a toddler, and yet she knew, even if her motor skills were functional, she wouldn't be able to pull away anyway.

Like last night, he didn't take the time to be gentle. He parted her lips with his tongue then shoved it inside her mouth, while his hands drifted down to her waist to keep her against him. And just when she began to respond, just when her tongue flicked against his and the fingers of her right hand slid into his dark hair, he pulled back.

And grinned at her.

"Know what that was?" he said cheerfully.

She struggled to catch her breath. "A totally insensitive way to shut me up?"

"Our first fight." He dropped his hands from her hips and stuck them back in his pockets. "So, when are you off work, Red?"

All she could do was stare at him. Were all movie stars this crazy or was it just this particular one?

"I'm done at two," she found herself replying. "Why?"

He ignored the question. "I'll meet you here when you're done. You can give me your answer then."

She swallowed. "My answer?"

"About letting me stay with you."

"I already said—"

He pressed his index finger to her lips, which caused a shiver to dance up her spine. "Think about it. That's all I ask. Give me your answer after you've had a chance to do that." He shot her that cocky smile again. "Not that there's much to think about. You and I both know exactly where I'll be spending the night, don't we, Maggie?"

Chapter Four

Maggie would've really liked to come up with an indignant comeback to the cocky little remark Ben had tossed her way, but she had to go inside and finish her shift before she could think of something indignant enough.

In your dreams had been on the forefront of her brain, but not only did it sound totally juvenile, she had a feeling it wouldn't faze Ben Barrett, who hands down had to be the most arrogant man on the planet.

She was still shaking her head to herself when she reentered the bar, and not even the chattering crowd could distract her from her thoughts. A new musical had just opened at the theater down the street, and though Maggie found herself hurrying from table to table to cater to the post-show crowd, though her hands scribbled down orders and her legs carried her to the kitchen and back, her brain had other things to worry about.

Like what to say to Ben when she finished work.

No would be the smart response. *Yes*, of course, would be the stupid one. In fact, she could think of half a dozen reasons why saying *yes* would be a bad, *bad* idea.

One, Summer would never agree to it.

This could've been a super reason, if not for the fact that Summer wouldn't be there. She was staying at Tygue's for the rest of the weekend, and the couple was leaving for Jamaica early Monday morning, which meant Maggie would have the place to herself for eight days...

"Don't even think it," she muttered to herself.

"What's wrong with a strawberry daiquiri?"

Realizing she'd spoken out loud, Maggie shot a reassuring look to the balding, middle-aged man sitting at one of her booths. "What? Oh, nothing's wrong, sir. The strawberry daiquiri is delicious."

"Wayne, she's trying to tell you it's not manly," the man's female companion grumbled. "Order a beer, for God's sake."

Wayne set his jaw. "I'm having a daiquiri, Jeannine."

The duo began arguing about masculine versus feminine drinks, and Maggie slinked away, the bickering couple all but forgotten as she resumed her mental list of reasons to tell Ben to get lost.

Two, she didn't even know him. He was famous, sure, but not to her. How could she be sure he wasn't an axe murderer who hid behind his celebrity status while he hacked silly waitresses to pieces?

There, try to challenge that one, she told that little voice in her head. The voice stayed quiet, but Maggie could tell it was unfazed.

She headed for the counter, still deep in thought.

Three, he was arrogant.

And then there was reason number four—he was a good kisser.

And why is this bad?

Well, because his high-caliber kissing skills would be nothing but a distraction. She didn't have time for distractions. Her exams were coming up. She needed to study. Needed to focus. Needed...

Sex.

She mentally chided her hormones for raising their voice, but she had to admit they brought up a good point. First, her night with Tony hadn't panned out, then she'd found herself in Ben's bed—which had only deepened that sexual ache—and now, after the hot kiss he'd planted on her outside, the ache was even worse.

"You look busy."

Maggie glanced up in surprise as Summer approached the counter. Setting a martini glass down on her tray, she pushed all thoughts of Ben and sex and sex with Ben out of her mind, and smiled at her roommate.

"Hey! What brings you here?"

"I came to say goodbye."

"You're not leaving 'til Monday."

Summer shrugged and ran a hand through her stick-straight blonde hair. "Yeah, but I'll be at Tygue's tonight and tomorrow, so I figured I'd say goodbye now."

Looking around, Maggie spotted Linda and met the older woman's eyes. "Break?" she mouthed. She gestured to Summer, who'd been Linda's pet when she'd waitressed at the bar.

With a nod, Linda waved at Summer, then held up five fingers, indicating the number of minutes Maggie could steal away for. Normally she never took unscheduled breaks, but since Summer was here, she might as well squeeze some advice out of her level-headed friend.

They headed for the employee lounge in the back, where Maggie flopped down on the ugly plaid couch and reached down to rub her sore ankles. "You're so lucky you quit," she grumbled, dreading how much worse her feet would feel when her shift finally ended.

"Don't worry, you'll get your degree soon and leave this place too." Summer leaned against the arm of the couch and eyed her expectantly. "So what's up? Did you bring me back here for a private goodbye kiss?"

"I need your help."

"What'd you do?"

"Nothing," Maggie said, insulted. "I just need you to talk me out of something."

Oh God, was this how close she'd come to agreeing to Ben's request? She'd thought she'd done a good job sifting through the cons, that when she saw him again after work the word "no" would fly out of her mouth as easy as the bad notes flew from Summer's drum.

Why was her resolve faltering now?

"Remember my stranger from last night?" she said with a sigh.

Summer grinned. "How could I forget?"

"Well, he's no longer a stranger. He showed up today."

A gasp came barreling out of Summer's throat. "No! He actually tracked you down? Why?"

"He said he wanted to see me."

"Well, that's nice of him."

She stared at her friend. "You don't find that the least bit strange?"

"Strange? No. I think it's kind of sweet."

Maggie snorted. "Trust me. He's not sweet. He's arrogant and presumptuous and—"

"You like him."

She replied with a dirty look and a stubborn silence.

"Is it so bad, actually liking someone?" Summer teased. "Just go on a date with him, see what happens."

"He doesn't want a date," she said through clenched teeth. "He wants to have a sleepover."

"A sleepover? You mean—ohhhh." Summer's eyes lit up. "So what the hell are you grumbling about? You said he was gorgeous, you two had chemistry, why not dub him the new Tony?"

"Because he's *not* Tony. He's demanding and complicated."

"So maybe you need demanding and complicated. When was the last time you got involved with a guy without calling the shots?" Summer frowned. "I get you have goals, Mags, but that's no reason to stop having fun. If I were you, I'd totally be up for a sleepover."

Summer stood up and smoothed down the front of her pink A-line skirt. "I've gotta go. Tygue's waiting for me outside."

"What?" Maggie shot to her feet. "You can't go. You never talked me out of anything."

"And I don't intend to." Flipping her hair over her shoulder, Summer headed for the door.

"Wait," she called after her friend. "One more thing."

With a sigh, Summer turned around. "What now?"

"Do you know anything about an actor named Ben Barrett?"

"Hmmm...I think he was in that movie Tygue and I rented last week. He played this ex-SWAT member who had to save an old flame from a group of arms dealers."

"Is he an axe murderer?"

"What? No. I just told you, he played a SWAT—"

"Not the character. The actor." Maggie knew she was grasping at straws. "Have you ever heard anything about him
66

being dangerous?"

"Why on earth are you asking me this?"

"Um, Trisha. She thought she saw him on the news for whacking someone." Dear God, was she this desperate to find a reason not to let Ben stay at her place?

"Whacking? Oh, you mean, like mafia or something?" Summer chewed on her bottom lip. "I don't think so. Only thing I know about the guy is that women love him."

Wonderful.

"You want my advice, Mags?" Summer added. "Stop thinking about Trisha and movie stars, and have sex with your stranger already. You know you want to, so quit griping and just do it."

"Just do it," she muttered to herself. "Like the condom ad."

"Nike."

"Huh?"

"Shoes, Maggie!" Summer's eyes darkened with disbelief. "That does it. You're so absorbed with work and school that you've lost touch with the rest of the world. Look, do me favor and spend some time with a man who won't fly to Fiji the second he zips up his pants. Tygue and I will be gone for a week, so maybe take advantage of that empty apartment and allow a few complications to murk up your life, okay? It'll be good for you."

Women didn't say no to Ben Barrett.

It was simply one of those delicious facts of life that Ben had come to accept over the years. He was fifteen when he first realized the power he had over women. Fifteen when a few friends dared him to ask the most popular senior girl in school to the freshman prom, and not only had Ben walked into the high school gym with the hottest girl on his arm, but he'd also lost his virginity that night.

Needless to say, he wasn't surprised when Maggie walked out of the bar at two a.m. and gestured for him to follow her.

Oh yeah, he still had a way with the ladies. They just couldn't say no.

Yet while this fiery redhead was no exception, she *was* the first female he'd encountered who had the nerve to look less than pleased with her decision to say yes.

"I'm not going to stay at your place if you sulk all night," he said, keeping his stride casual as he followed her down the sidewalk.

It was late, and the Saturday night crowds had finally started to disperse. In the distance, a thin mist shrouded the buildings and skyscrapers, and the spring air was chilled, causing Ben to zip up his leather jacket. When he glanced over at Maggie, he was pleased to see her nipples poking against the thin bra under the blue long-sleeved shirt she now wore. She'd also changed into a pair of snug blue jeans and tied her long red hair into a low ponytail, which made her seem younger.

If it weren't for the frown on her face, she might have looked a little sweeter too.

"I'm not sulking," she replied, the frown deepening.

"Sure you are." He stuck his hands in his pockets and cocked his head at her. "I actually find it quite insulting."

She stopped walking. "You want to know what's insulting? You assuming you can waltz into my life and expect me to agree to whatever tickles your fancy."

He lifted a brow. "Considering we're on the way to your apartment, I'd say that wasn't a bad assumption."

Her cheeks turned bright red. "The only reason I'm letting you stay over is because I feel sorry for you," she huffed.

A laugh trickled out of his mouth. "Sure, babe. If you say so."

They fell into step again, Ben still chuckling to himself and Maggie apparently using silence as punishment for his amusement. He wondered how she'd react if he told her he viewed her silence as a reward. If he told her she was the first woman who didn't chatter his ear off. Or coddle him. Or try to seduce him to further her own ambitions.

Not that he didn't like being seduced. Every now and then, however, he liked the challenge of doing the seducing himself, a rare feat, considering most women were ready to fuck him before he even asked. Hell, these days he didn't even have to ask.

"This is it," Maggie said, finally breaking the drawn-out silence as they came to a stop in front of an older-looking high-rise with large balconies.

She used a key to get into the lobby, then headed for the elevator without looking back to see if he was following. It was kinda cute, the way she pretended she was doing him a favor by letting him come home with her. He knew better, of course. The way she'd trembled against him during the kiss they'd shared earlier proved the attraction between them was so very mutual.

"So how long have you lived here?" he asked casually as they stepped into the elevator car.

Maggie shot him a dirty look. "Don't make small talk."

Taken aback, he said, "Why not?"

"Because you're only wasting time." The doors opened with a loud buzzing noise, and Maggie whisked out of the car, over her shoulder adding, "Neither of us has any illusions about why you're here."

Again her words startled him, so much so that the elevator nearly closed on his toes. He pushed forward before the doors shut and hurried after Maggie. Another first, having to chase after a woman.

"And what's that supposed to mean?" He caught up to her right as she unlocked the door to her apartment and strolled in.

"It means we both know how this night is going to end," she replied, mocking him with his earlier words.

Any other time Ben would have had a sexy comeback, but the second he entered Maggie's apartment, he became speechless.

"This is where you live?" he asked, gaping.

"Yeah. Is there a problem?"

There wasn't a problem, per se, but Ben certainly hadn't expected these surroundings. If he hadn't seen Maggie unlock the door, he would've thought they were in the wrong apartment.

The place looked like somebody's grandmother lived in it. Furniture, mostly plaid upholstery, all mismatched. The paintings on the wall depicted bland landscapes and the occasional kitten rolling around in a garden. Frilly pink tablecloths and doilies that looked handmade covered every table in the room, and Ben had to blink a few times to be sure, but he thought he saw photos of Cary Grant and a young Marlon Brando hanging over the television set.

The only item in the apartment that resembled anything modern was the steel drum sitting in the open-concept dining room, but he couldn't quite figure *that* out either.

When he finished his wide-eyed scrutiny, he glanced over and saw the humor dancing in Maggie's green eyes.

"C'mon, say it," she taunted.

"What?"

"How tacky it is. We both know you want to say it."

He might've been living in Hollywood for the last ten years of his life, but he'd grown up in Ohio with a mother who'd instilled good manners in him. "It's not tacky," he lied, hoping his tone sounded polite. "Did you decorate it yourself?"

Laughter bubbled out of her delicate throat. "Wow. Did you learn the art of bullshitting from the film industry or does it just come naturally to you?"

"What? No, I think this place is really something."

She laughed again, louder this time. "Relax, Ben. I didn't decorate it. My roommate, Summer, her grandmother owns this place. When she moved, she made Summer promise not to change a thing."

His ears perked. "You have a roommate?"

Maggie's amused expression quickly transformed into another frown. "Summer's gone for the week—and she has a boyfriend. So wipe any notion of a threesome out of your head."

How was it humanly possible that she kept catching him off-guard like this?

His nostrils flared as he pondered the best way to respond. Screw good manners. A remark like that merited nothing less than irate indignation.

"You really don't think much of me, do you?" he returned, steel in his voice.

"I don't even know you." Apparently she was just as capable of steely tones.

"You're right, you don't." Eyes narrowing, he added, "The reason I asked about your roommate is because I wanted to make sure we'd be alone."

"Well, we are." She crossed her arms over her chest and

sighed. "So let's just do this, okay?"

"Do what?"

"Let's have sex."

"No thanks." He unzipped his jacket and shrugged it off his shoulders. "So, should I sleep on the couch or is there a spare room?"

"Excuse me?" She dropped her arms and let them dangle at her sides. "Did you just say 'no thanks'?"

He tossed his jacket on a nearby armchair. "That's right, I did."

When he met her gaze, she had the gall to look confused. "You don't want to have sex?"

"Not when you act like it's a chore."

Another sigh tumbled out of her mouth, longer this time, and lined with exasperation. "I can't believe you. You've been flirting with me all night, taunting me with how we're going to end up in bed together, and when I finally give in, you back out. Unbelievable!"

Shaking her head, she stalked past him and flew into the kitchen. A large window had been cut out of the wall, so he could see her every movement as she pulled the fridge door open so hard the items on the shelves clattered against one another. Ben hid a grin, enjoying the way she grabbed a carton of orange juice and slammed it on the counter.

She looked pissed and he loved it. Not that he got off on infuriating women, but this one deserved to have a few feathers ruffled. He was used to people assuming things about him, but Maggie was the first woman who'd ever openly challenged and criticized him. The first woman who acted like having sex with him was as appealing as a root canal.

"Why did you ask me to come here when it's obviously not

what you want?" He knew he sounded angry, but what annoyed him more was the faint twinge of disappointment he heard in his voice. If anyone should be disappointed, it was her.

She poured a glass of orange juice and then sipped the liquid slowly, as if contemplating her answer. He noticed that the fire had left her eyes, replaced by a flicker of hesitation.

"It is what I want," she finally replied.

Her entire demeanor was so glum that his ego took a nice hit. "You sound so enthusiastic."

She tightened her lips. "You don't get it." Turning around, she moved to the far end of the kitchen.

He couldn't see her from where he stood, but he heard the sound of running water, then her soft footsteps as she returned to the main room. She played with the edge of her ponytail and the vulnerability dancing across her fair face chipped away at his anger.

"I don't have much room in my life for dating." She gave a self-deprecating smile. "Or sex, for that matter."

"And yet our first meeting took place in a hotel room, with you getting naked and hopping into my bed." He took a step closer, but still kept a few feet between them. "Who were you supposed to meet, by the way?"

"Tony." Her reply came out as a groan.

The spark of jealousy he felt at the sound of another man's name on Maggie's lips was not only unwelcome, but bewildering. "And who's Tony?"

She stared down at her high heels as if they were the most interesting thing she'd seen in days. "Just a guy I meet a couple times a year."

Ben faltered. "Not a boyfriend?"

"No. Like I said, I don't have time for dating. Or sex," she repeated.

As understanding dawned, Ben couldn't fight an amazed laugh. "Are you saying you only have sex two times a year, with this Tony guy?"

"Sometimes it's three," she said, sounding defensive.

Another laugh tickled his throat. He tried very hard to swallow it back. For the first time all night Maggie had dropped her combative attitude. The last thing he wanted was to spark another fight by making fun of her, though in his defense, the laughter lodged in his throat was yet again driven by amazement, not ridicule.

"What exactly keeps you so busy?" he asked, genuinely curious.

She shrugged. "Work. School. Volunteering. And relationships always seem to get in the way."

"I see."

"That's why I don't understand *this*," she blurted.

"This?"

"You and me. The attraction, whatever." She rubbed her forehead with one hand, then her temples, then pinched the bridge of her nose, as if acknowledging the chemistry between them was nothing but a headache. "I don't bring guys to my apartment. I don't have flings. I don't have *time* for flings. Especially with men like you."

Against his better sense, a grin lifted the corners of his mouth. "And what kind of man am I?"

She bit on her lip. "The complicated kind. The distracting kind."

His grin widened. "What is it about me that distracts you?" He closed the distance between them, planting his hands on her waist. "Let me guess. My rugged good looks? Or maybe it's the way I kiss?"

"Ben—"

"No, wait, I figured it out." He brushed his finger over her lips, pleased when he heard her sharp inhale. "I distract you because—much as it bugs you—I turn you on like no man ever has. Isn't that right, Maggie?"

"No."

He chuckled. "It's okay to be in denial. And it's also okay to feel disappointed."

She pushed his hand off her mouth and stepped back. "Why would I feel disappointed?"

"Because the ship has sailed, babe."

"What ship?"

"The sex ship." He crossed his arms over his chest. "You blew it, Red."

"Excuse me?" Both her reddish-brown eyebrows sailed up to her forehead, and Ben felt like kissing that indignant frown off her sexy mouth.

But he didn't.

"You heard me. You missed your chance." He poked the inside of his cheek with his tongue and fought back a grin. "I'm sorry to inform you I won't be fucking you tonight."

"You are the most *arrogant*—"

"Enough small talk," he cut in with a pleasant smile. "Will you be showing me to my room or should I just take the couch?"

Chapter Five

Was it possible to hate a man and want to rip off his clothes at the same time?

Maggie had pondered the question for hours, but the answer still eluded her. What remained crystal clear, however, was that if there was a one-to-ten scale of sexual frustration, she'd be sitting at eleven right about now.

As the late morning sunlight streamed in from the open window blinds, she slid up into a sitting position and leaned against the headboard, wondering if Ben had slept as horribly as she had. Probably not. Knowing him, he'd dreamt about kittens and rainbows all night long, unfazed by everything that happened.

She, on the other hand, had spent eight hours tossing and turning and fighting the urge to jump out of bed and jump Ben Barrett's bones.

God, she'd acted like a spoiled brat last night.

Try bitch.

Fine, so she'd call a spade a spade.

When she'd brought Ben back to the apartment, she truly had intended to follow Summer's advice and have some fun. Easier said than done. They'd walked inside, and the first thing she'd seen was the pile of textbooks on the computer desk. The stack of bills on the hall table. The schedule tacked up on the fridge.

Then she'd looked over and there was Ben. A big sexy man who made it clear he wanted to tear off her clothes with his teeth. A big sexy man who kissed like a champion and made her feel dizzy with desire.

That's when the confusion kicked in. Somehow this cocky movie star managed to make important tasks like studying and earning a degree in social work seem secondary, and her body's eagerness to betray her life's goals had absolutely floored her.

To make matters worse, after she'd let down her guard and admitted she didn't usually make time for sex, Ben had backed off. Just when she'd been ready to stop acting like an uptight party-pooper—fine, bitch—he'd promptly taken sex off the table and gone to bed. Alone.

What was up with that?

Yawning, Maggie glanced at the digital clock on her bedside table. Ten-thirty. She couldn't remember the last time she'd gotten up later than eight, and the knowledge that she'd wasted half her morning stewing over Ben's rejection and her own stupidity wasn't one she liked waking up with.

The faint sound of music finally drew her out of her warm covers. She wrinkled her forehead as she searched for her slippers, the fuzzy pink cat ones the kids at the community center had collectively bought her last year for her birthday. She found them in front of the closet, slipped them onto her bare feet and left the bedroom.

In the narrow hall, the music grew louder. Sounded like...The Beach Boys? Yep, The Beach Boys, she realized as the soft strains of "I Get Around" became clear. Then she made out a male voice humming along and nearly burst out laughing.

Priceless. Ben Barrett listening to "I Get Around". Probably his life's theme song.

She found him in the kitchen, frying eggs over the stove and singing along with the stereo, which he'd brought in from the living room and set up right on the splintered cedar work island in the middle of the room. The Beach Boys CD, of course, belonged to Summer, who still hadn't mastered any of the songs on her drum.

She opened her mouth to utter a crack about making himself at home, but the words died in her throat the second he turned around.

He stood there, barefoot and bare-chested, wearing nothing but a pair of jeans that rode low on his lean hips. His dark hair demonstrated a serious case of bedhead, and the stubble on his chin was thicker, giving him a masculine sexiness that caused arousal to simmer in her belly.

Her gaze drifted to his tattoo, the tribal design that turned her heartbeat into a thumping tribal drum. Her pulse quickened as she glanced south again and noted the absence of a second waistband. Was he not wearing any boxers? That realization alone was enough to soak her cotton panties.

God, why did this man have to be so damn...*sexable*?

"Finished gawking?"

His rough voice caused her to snap her head up. He was grinning at her, looking totally pleased by the fact that she'd been checking him out.

"I wasn't gawking," she lied, breezing toward the fridge and getting out the orange juice. "I was just—"

"Shhh." He held up his hand to silence her, cocked his head toward the stereo, and started singing the first few lines of "Barbara Ann".

Open-mouthed, Maggie just stared at him, waiting until he

tired of the song and turned his attention back to the sunny-side eggs sizzling in the pan.

"I take it you're a Beach Boys fan," she said, sipping her juice. She then set down the glass so she could run her fingers through her frizzy, slept-on hair.

It was slightly unnerving having him here, making breakfast in nothing but a pair of jeans. She and Tony never did the breakfast thing, or the morning thing, or any *thing* that didn't involve hot sex followed by goodbye.

"The biggest," he replied, shooting her a toe-curling grin before reaching over to turn off the stove.

Using a spatula, he dropped one egg on a plate, followed by a piece of brown toast, and handed it to her. "Enjoy."

When was the last time a man had cooked for her?

Oh right. Never.

Oddly touched, she took the plate, then the fork he held out, and settled on the lone stool by the counter. The kitchen was too small to be considered eat-in on any real estate listing, and Maggie was about to suggest moving to the dining room table when Ben picked up his own plate, leaned against the counter, and started eating standing up. Well. At least he wasn't one of those celebrities who expected to be served while he sat on a throne.

"You know, I dated a girl named Barbara Ann once," he said after he'd swallowed a bite of toast.

"Doesn't surprise me." She chewed slowly. "I bet you've also dated a Rhonda, and every other girl the Beach Boys sing about. You've also dated every actress and model in the eighteen to thirty-five demographic."

"What makes you say that?"

"I Googled you last night."

"No, you didn't. We slept in separate bedrooms."

She rolled her eyes. "Google, as in the Internet search engine, wise guy. I couldn't sleep, so I researched you."

He polished off the rest of his meal and walked over to the sink. To her surprise, he washed his dish and set it to dry on the plastic tray on the counter, then left the frying pan in the sink to soak. Wow. Even Summer didn't do her dishes this quickly, and Maggie had dubbed her the ultimate neat-freak.

"Why couldn't you sleep?" Ben asked, seemingly oblivious to the rest of her admission.

"I just told you I researched you and you want to know why I couldn't sleep?"

"Yep." He grinned. "So why couldn't you?"

I was too busy fantasizing about licking every inch of your body. "I was too tired."

"Right." It was obvious he didn't believe her.

"Anyway," she went on, hoping he'd leave it at that, "it turns out you're quite the playboy."

He looked insulted. "I'm not a playboy."

"Sure you are. You travel the world and have casual affairs with gorgeous women. That makes you a playboy."

She didn't mention that unwelcome pang of jealousy she'd experienced while reading about Ben Barrett's conquests. Of all the things that annoyed her since Ben had insinuated his way into her life, the jealousy topped the list. Considering the only type of appearance Ben would be making in her world would be a cameo, she had no idea what to make of the claws that came out when she'd seen all those photos of him with other women.

"Well, with you getting laid only twice a year, I can see why my reputation might intimidate you," Ben teased.

"Sometimes three times," she corrected. Then she scowled.

"You really are one of those annoyingly cheerful morning people, aren't you?"

"I sure am."

He waited while she shoved the last mouthful of eggs into her mouth, and then took her plate. To her surprise, he washed it as well.

"Don't tell me you dated a Martha Stewart too," she said with a sigh.

He wiped his hands with a pink dishcloth. "No, but I grew up with one. My mother never let me leave the kitchen until it was spotless."

As if to confirm that, he used the dishcloth to wipe the counter until it squeaked. When he finished, he turned to face her. "So what are we doing today?"

He caught her momentarily off guard, but she quickly covered up her surprise. "Well, I have a ton of stuff to do, and you, I assume, will be finding a hotel. Or maybe you'll be talking with your publicity people about your recent scandal. I read about that too, by the way."

His cheerful expression faded. "You did?"

"Yep," she mimicked. "So that rich lady left you her money, huh?"

She hit a nerve. She could tell from the way his features hardened and his eyes narrowed into slits. Not that she had a clue why she'd brought it up in the first place. Thanks to her mediocre Internet-searching skills, she'd only managed to dig up a few details about Ben's involvement with Gretchen Goodrich, but enough to suspect how touchy a subject it must be.

Goodrich, heiress to a salad dressing empire and wife of an Academy Award-winning director, had lost the battle with breast cancer three months ago, and from what Maggie read, she'd left Ben close to ten million dollars in her will. The press hinted at an affair between Ben and the fifty-three-year-old heiress, but since there was no evidence or confirmation of that, Maggie had decided it was most likely a rumor. Still, Ben must have been pretty close to the woman if she'd left him a part of her fortune...

"You can't believe everything you read," Ben said in a mild tone. The frown left his face, but his stiff posture said he was still on edge.

Before she could say anything else, he breezed past her, bare feet padding against the tiled floor. She figured he would head for Summer's room to get dressed, so when he flopped down on the living room couch and reached for the remote control, she bolted to her feet and scurried into the living room.

"What are you doing?" she demanded. "I just told you, I've got tons of stuff to do."

"I'll wait." He flipped on the TV and turned it to ESPN.

"You can't wait," she said, exasperation climbing up her chest. "I have a really busy day."

Ben pressed the mute button and shot her an expectant look. "Doing what?"

"You want me to write you a list?"

"No, a verbal break-down would be fine."

Oh, she'd give him a verbal break-down, all right. She didn't care how sexy he looked in those jeans or how enticing his chest was. It was Sunday, and Sunday was *her* day. The only day she didn't work or volunteer or take notes in a classroom. Sure, she spent the free time studying and doing homework, but it was free time nonetheless.

"I have to finish writing a paper," she said, setting her jaw.

"Then I have to research child abuse law and make notes so I can write another paper. *Then* I need to study for my exams." She took a breath. "And after I've done all that, I was going to wax my legs. Satisfied?"

He furrowed his dark brows. "Why do you wax your legs when the only guy who sees them comes to town twice a year?"

"Sometimes three times," she snapped. "And I don't need to justify my leg-waxing routines to you. So get dressed and go do some movie star things like, I don't know, golfing or staring at your reflection in store windows."

The laugh he gave sounded like honeyed sandpaper. "Is that what you think movie stars do?"

"I don't care what you do," she replied, starting to grow annoyed. "I just want you to go away. My schoolwork requires silence."

"So I'll be quiet." He shrugged and directed his attention back to the sports highlight reel flashing across the TV screen.

It took all her willpower not to pull her own hair out by the roots. What did he *want* from her? Obviously not sex, considering he hadn't touched her since last night.

"You're seriously not going to leave?" Her voice was a cross between a squeak and a groan, with a growl thrown in for good measure.

Ben's blue eyes never left the screen. "Nope."

"But...I...you...just keep the volume down!"

Spinning on her heel, she stormed into her bedroom and cursed herself for not being strong enough to physically throw him out.

As she got dressed, she heard him chuckling from the other room.

Because he'd taken a vow of silence, Ben spent most of the afternoon fighting back soundless laughter and watching television with the volume off and the captions on. In the dining room, Maggie sat at her small desk, typing away on the computer keyboard and stopping every now and then to rustle through the pages of a textbook the size of an encyclopedia.

She'd been working for hours, her eyes glued to the monitor, her fingers on the keyboard, and the way she kept biting her bottom lip in concentration made Ben want to walk over there and capture that plump lip with his teeth.

He wasn't quite sure why he was forcing his presence on her, especially after last night. If any other woman had grumbled that much about the idea of fucking him, he'd have shook her hand, said goodbye and moved on.

This morning he'd asked himself if pursuing a woman who viewed sex as a complication was worth the hassle. He had nothing against playing hard to get, but in Maggie's case, it went beyond a coy little game. She seemed genuinely annoyed with him. And what was the deal with her whole 'I have sex twice a year' declaration?

Their night at the Lester Hotel proved she was a passionate woman, so why did she save all that passion for that loser Tony, a guy who offered a few clandestine trysts a year?

Under normal circumstances, Ben would pass on the challenge and focus his energy on a woman who actually wanted to be around him, but there was nothing normal about this situation. Or about Maggie.

Since he'd met her, he'd barely thought about the recent scandal hanging over his head, or the fact that reporters were camped outside his home. Because of Maggie, he'd managed to think about something other than his own troubles, and he wanted to hang on to that liberating feeling for a while longer.

Like he'd told his agent, he would lay low, and truth be told, he couldn't think of anyone else he wanted to lay low with than this sassy redhead, no matter how annoying she found him.

"You should take a break." He spoke before he could stop himself, hoping Maggie wouldn't reprimand him for breaking his oath of silence.

"I just have to write up my conclusion," she said absently without turning around. She rapped a few keys with her fingers. "Give me a sec."

He tried to tell himself he wasn't thinking of his own needs as he rose from the couch and walked toward her. Instead, he focused on the fact that Maggie had been working for five hours straight without so much as a bathroom break.

Standing behind her, he placed his hands on her shoulders and started rubbing the knot between her shoulder blades. She flinched for a second and then leaned into his massaging fingers, sighing softly.

"See, you need a break," he chided. "You're so stiff."

And boy, did he know what stiff felt like. Although the material of her green long-sleeved shirt was woven from thick cotton, he could feel the heat of her skin underneath his fingertips. From there, his mind played a torturous game of *What other parts of her body are hot?* Her breasts? Her thighs? Her—

"I can feel you poking against my back, by the way." The chair's backrest left a gap between her lower back and shoulders, and she wiggled her tailbone against his growing erection.

Her teasing voice brought the warmth of embarrassment to his cheeks. Jesus. He was Ben Barrett. He didn't get embarrassed when he sprang a boner.

"Don't act like you're not getting wet feeling me against

you," he growled.

"Wet? No. But I am a little hungry. Should we order a pizza?"

Some primitive part of him made him swivel the chair, determined to prove to this woman that his aroused state turned her on as much as it did him. Her eyes widened as he sank to his knees and dipped both hands under the waistband of her black fleece track pants.

"What are you doing?" She practically squeaked out the question. "I told you I have work to do."

"And I told you it's time to take a break." He forcibly lifted her ass off the chair so he could peel her pants off her legs, running his hands over her as each smooth inch of skin was revealed. "You don't need to wax your legs," he murmured as he tossed the track pants aside.

She sighed. "I know. I lied."

His mouth lifted in a grin, partly because of her admission, partly because that agitated look on her face was completely foreign on her. Since he'd met her, she'd been cool and composed, her green eyes flashing with fire on occasion, her cheeks reddening with arousal. He liked it all, but not as much as he enjoyed the vulnerability and raw desire currently expressed on her dainty features.

He continued to stroke her legs, and then moved his hands north again. Touching the damp crotch of her bright yellow panties, he managed a chuckle. "Told you you're wet."

"You're imagining it."

He dragged his fingers up to her waistband.

She groaned and tried to wriggle away from his caress. "I don't have time for this," she grumbled.

"Sure you do."

"I have homework..."

"It can wait."

Before she could object further, he removed her panties and threw them out of her reach, then lowered his head and placed a soft kiss on her clit.

She gasped.

Then sighed.

Then moaned.

Fighting back a smile, he kissed her again, and again, and again, until it dawned on him that he wasn't out to prove a point anymore. He'd intended to show her she couldn't hide the effect he had on her and prove the attraction between them was oh so mutual. But as he ran his tongue over her wet pussy, he forgot about all that.

She tasted like heaven. He swirled lazy figure-eights over her clit, savoring the sweet taste of her, groaning against her when she released a whimper of pleasure and widened her legs. If his cock wasn't throbbing relentlessly and his head wasn't buzzing with lust, he might have kept up the slow pace.

As it was, all he could do was speed up, suddenly anxious to bring her over the edge and make her scream his name as she came.

The wish was fulfilled a lot faster than he'd expected. All it took was for him to slide one finger deep inside her pussy and suck her clit hard in his mouth, and she shuddered with an orgasm so powerful he almost came in his pants.

She wasn't one of those women who bit her lip and writhed in silent pleasure. Oh no. Maggie vocalized every sexy second of her climax. Moaning. Trembling. Even tossing out an *oh fuck* or two as she tangled her fingers in his hair and locked her thighs around his head.

When she finally whimpered and grew still, Ben pulled back, a satisfied grin on his face and an unsatisfied erection straining against his zipper.

"You don't play fair," Maggie murmured, cheeks flushed, eyes a little glazed.

"Never have," he returned easily. He gave her inner thigh a light pinch and got to his feet, liking her disheveled appearance because he was responsible for it. "All right. I'm hopping into the shower. You can go ahead and finish your homework now."

So he wanted to play games? Was that it? Maggie wondered as she stared at Ben's sexy backside disappearing into the hallway.

She inhaled a deep breath, then stumbled off the chair and bent down to retrieve her panties from the floor. She was still a little stunned by what happened, and more than a little shaky from the exquisite orgasm that had just rocked her world.

Ben Barrett had made her come in a record-breaking three minutes. He hadn't asked her what she liked. Hadn't waited for her to guide him. He simply *knew*. It didn't surprise her. The second she'd slid into bed with him two nights ago she'd known this man possessed the ability to set her body on fire.

He'd taken advantage of that ability just a minute ago, making sure, of course, that she'd never be able to concentrate on schoolwork now.

It was hard to stand up when her core still throbbed from Ben's erotic assault, but Maggie forced herself to her feet. She walked toward the bathroom on shaky legs, her determination deepening when she heard the shower running.

If he wanted to play games, she was ready to play back. If only to give her aroused body what it wanted so she could finish researching her paper without any distractions.

At least that's what she told herself as she turned the doorknob and stepped into the small, steam-filled bathroom. The bright pink plastic curtain shielded Ben from her view, and her from his, but she slid out of her clothes quietly, needing to hold on to the upper hand. She'd nearly melted into a puddle on the floor from Ben's skilled tongue, but this time he'd be the one melting.

"Are you joining me or what?" His muffled voice broke through the sound of water flowing.

Her nostrils flared. Damn it. She didn't even have the element of surprise on her side. How had he known she'd follow him in here? Was he so arrogant that he just assumed she'd run into the washroom to get a glimpse of his naked body?

It's what you did, isn't it?

She pushed that annoying voice out of her head and reached for the edge of the shower curtain. As she pulled it open, a billow of steam clouded her vision and made her slightly light-headed. When it cleared, her eyes focused, but she was just as light-headed, because the sight of Ben, wet, hard and naked, was enough to suck all the oxygen out of her lungs.

Her brain went into overload trying to absorb all the delicious little details. Like his smooth, golden skin. And his rippled abs. And those firm, muscular thighs. And his...oh, gosh, his *everything*.

"You're letting the cold air in," he complained.

She swallowed, trying to regain her composure, then took a breath and stepped into the shower stall. The second she did, he shoved his hands on her bare hips, pulled her into the stream of water pouring from the showerhead and captured her lips with his.

He gave her another one of those rough, drugging kisses, but this time she broke the contact before she could completely lose herself in his lips.

"I don't like being interrupted from my work," she murmured, leaning on her tiptoes and pressing her lips to his ear so he could hear her over the rush of water.

He raised his brow, sending droplets of moisture down his aristocratic nose and into the thick stubble on his chin.

"Okay. Should I apologize for stealing you away from your desk and making you come?"

"No." She ran her hand over his wet chest. One flat, brown nipple hardened beneath her fingers. "I'm just voicing my disapproval."

"So, what, you crashed my shower to punish me?" One side of his mouth lifted upwards in a crooked grin. His metallic blue eyes smoldered when he said the word "punish".

"Something like that."

She glided her hand down his chest and encircled his shaft.

He inhaled, eyes widening then narrowing with arousal. Drops of water pooled over his upper lip and, feeling bold, Maggie leaned forward and licked the moisture off with her tongue. She met his gaze and offered a crooked grin of her own, then slid to her knees and took his cock in her mouth.

This time his sharp intake of breath was followed by a low groan. His hands drifted down and tangled in her hair, which had matted against her forehead from the steam. She pushed a few wet strands out of her eyes and licked him from base to tip, enjoying his velvety texture and masculine taste.

And, unlike Ben, she took her time teasing him. Tortured him with long languid strokes of her tongue and pulled back each time he tried to thrust deeper. She dragged her lips over his tip, sucking, kissing, stroking his balls with her palm.

His husky moans and the feel of the hot water streaming

over her breasts drove her crazy. She clamped her knees together and tried to focus on bringing him to the edge, until he tugged at her hair and she looked up to meet his heavy-lidded gaze.

"Touch yourself," he ordered, his words hissing through the steam filling the small space. "I want to see you touch yourself."

She swallowed back a whimper and nodded. Widening her knees, she pressed her fingers between her legs and took him in her mouth again. Going slow was no longer an option, not when she could feel Ben watching her as she rubbed her clit, not when she could feel his thick cock pulsing under her tongue.

They came together, hard, fast. His semen filled her mouth and she swallowed every last drop, while her own orgasm sizzled her nerve endings, bringing with it a wave of pleasure that numbed every part of her body. With a ragged groan, Ben gently pushed her head back and sank to the floor of the tub, looking completely and thoroughly spent.

As the water from above grew lukewarm, he reached out and brushed hair out of her eyes, then stroked one of her trembling thighs. "You okay?"

She knew she must look like a drowned rat, still shaking from her climax and gasping for air, and she laughed at the concern she saw in his eyes. "I'm fine. Numb, but fine."

He grinned. "In case you're wondering, I'm fine too."

She glanced down at his crotch. He still sported a rock-hard erection, and she was shocked to feel her nipples harden with desire. *Again?* She'd just experienced her second orgasm in twenty minutes and she was ready to go again?

She wasn't sure what made her jump to her feet, that startling realization or the sudden change of water temperature, which went from lukewarm to lukecold. Whatever the reason, she quickly tugged on the shower curtain and stumbled onto the fluffy pink bathroom mat.

Ben called her name, but she ignored him.

Two days, she realized as she wrapped a terrycloth robe around her wet body and hurried out of the washroom. Two days since she'd first met Ben Barrett, two days of allowing him to distract her to no end, and now two orgasms that still hadn't managed to flush the man from her system.

What was the matter with her?

"What is the matter with you?" Ben sounded out of breath and annoyed as he marched into her bedroom a moment later wearing nothing but a towel.

She tightened the sash of her robe and crossed her arms over the thick terrycloth. "Nothing is the matter."

"So you always sprint out of a room after sex?"

"We didn't have sex."

Laughter spurted from his throat. "We came pretty damn close. In fact, we came pretty damn fast."

Her cheeks burned. "But we didn't cross the line."

A shadow floated across his face. "I wasn't even aware there was a line."

"Well, there is."

She felt unbearably exposed, standing there in her bathrobe, the hardwood floor icy under her bare feet. And unbelievably confused, because her mouth kept saying words that made Ben frown and her body kept berating her for it.

"So this line..." His frown turned into a scowl. "Is it the one that keeps you from having fun?"

"What?"

"You heard me. You crossed over from uptight land to fun world, and now you're trying to convince yourself what we did was wrong."

He was right, she *was* trying to convince herself they'd done something wrong, but not for the reason he believed. It had nothing to do with being uptight and everything to do with the way he made her feel.

Again, it all came down to distraction, and what happened when you let yourself get sidetracked by a man. She'd learned the hard way how easy it was for your life to be destroyed by a preoccupation with sex and relationships. Hell, her own mother had abandoned her because of a man, and though Maggie had no children of her own to abandon—which she would never do—she wasn't going to abandon the path she'd set up for herself. She wouldn't desert her goals and her dreams for a man. Even one who made her entire body tremble from one penetrating gaze.

"You think I'm uptight?" She decided to respond to the one remark he'd made that didn't hit close to home.

"Yep." He leaned one bare shoulder against the doorframe and cast a blue-eyed glare in her direction. "You're anti-fun, Red."

Irritation prickled her insides. "No, I'm not. I simply have different priorities than you."

"What's that supposed to mean?"

"It means my life doesn't revolve around fun. I have a job, I have goals, I have responsibilities. Unlike you, I don't have time to gallivant around, not if I want to pay my bills." Her jaw tightened. "I'm not as lucky as you, Ben. Ten million dollars doesn't just fall out of the sky and into my lap."

He made an exasperated sound. "I wasn't asking you to quit your job, Maggie. Only to let loose and enjoy your day off."

"Sorry, but I don't have that luxury. In my life there's no such thing as a day off."

Shaking his head, he edged away from the doorway. "Wow. Sounds like you lead a mighty fulfilling life," he cracked before disappearing into the hall.

"Ben," she called after him.

His footsteps stopped. "Yeah?"

She swallowed. "You should probably look for a hotel in the morning."

Chapter Six

Ben strode into the bedroom he'd slept in last night and let his towel drop to the floor. He was aggravated as hell, a reaction that came out in a string of mumbled expletives. Who could blame him? He'd just received an incredible blow job from an incredible woman who'd then turned around and told him to get lost. If that didn't merit a few four-letter words, what did?

You should probably look for a hotel.

Like hell he would.

He grabbed his T-shirt from the foot of the bed and put it on, then slid into his jeans without bothering with his boxers. Tomorrow he'd buy some new clothes. Until then he was going commando.

Maggie probably wouldn't even blink if she knew he wasn't wearing anything underneath his jeans. Why would she? It seemed like nothing he did would be enough to impress her.

It seriously pissed him off.

What the hell would it take to get under her skin? He'd thought the orgasm in the living room might do it. Or maybe the hot sex they could've shared if she hadn't run out of the shower like a frightened rabbit.

How was it possible that the one woman who'd intrigued him in a long time was also the one woman who wanted nothing to do with him? The chemistry between them was combustible enough to make anything it encountered burst into flames, but apparently chemistry didn't impress Maggie Reilly either. They'd barely had sex and already she was shooing him off the stage.

Of course, being the seasoned performer that he was, Ben had no intention of being shooed away.

Maybe it was the challenge, maybe infatuation, or maybe she simply represented some level of normalcy that had been missing from his life since he'd become famous. Whatever the reason, he couldn't walk away.

You should probably look for a hotel in the morning.

With those ten words, she'd thrown down the gauntlet, and no way would he come out the loser in this battle.

Running his fingers through his wet hair, he smothered a grin and left the bedroom.

When Maggie strode into the living room after she'd dressed and brushed her hair, she found it empty. The only signs of life came from the television Ben had left on, and *Entertainment Tonight* silently flashed across the screen.

He'd obviously gone without saying goodbye.

It shouldn't bother her, but it did.

"You're the one who told him to find a hotel," she muttered to herself, stretching out her legs and resting them on the coffee table.

She had, hadn't she? Right about now, every female in America would be screaming vile things at her if they knew she'd sent Ben Barrett away, but to hell with them.

Growing up, Maggie never felt like she belonged. At school, she'd been a loner. At home, she'd been invisible. It wasn't until she'd started volunteering at the Broger Center that she'd finally found a place where she fit in. She'd found her identity there, discovered that unwavering hunger to help the children and ensure they grew up feeling like they mattered.

As a kid, she'd been passed up for adoption so many times she'd given up on ever finding someone who truly cared about her. It was like being the last person picked for a game of softball. Standing there as everyone around you got picked one by one, feeling humiliated and unloved, as useless as a piece of trash on the sidewalk.

Only the stakes were higher than a silly sports game. It was about a child not being good enough to have parents.

It had taken her years to get past that pain and resentment, and she didn't want any of the kids she worked with to ever feel as alone as she had.

So what if it meant putting relationships on hold for a while? She wouldn't be single forever, just until she earned her degree. Then she'd go out and do what other women her age did. She'd date and flirt and maybe even get married. Other Ben Barretts would come along. It wasn't like saying goodbye to this one would have life-altering effects or anything, right?

"The ladies love Ben Barrett!"

Maggie yelped as Mary Hart's cheerful voice broke through the dismal silence in the room. Shifting, she felt the remote control dig into her butt and realized she'd accidentally pressed un-mute when she moved her legs.

She yanked the remote from under her, but couldn't bring herself to shut off the TV. Not when Ben's ridiculously sexy face mocked her from the screen. It was like driving past a gory car crash. You just couldn't look away.

"Bad boy Barrett might be stirring up some scandals recently, but the *Heart of a Hero* star still manages to stir up the ladies."

No kidding.

"Shanika Thomas, our New York correspondent, spent the day in the Big Apple chatting with Barrett's fans, who don't seem to mind all the negative attention their favorite celeb is receiving. In fact, it's unanimous—we all love him."

"Oh my God, Ben is sooooo cute!" a fan giggled into Shanika Thomas' microphone. "I don't care if he, like, slept with a married woman. He's still hot!"

"I'm a married woman and he can sure sleep with me," another fan remarked with a laugh. She lowered her voice. "Just don't tell my husband I said that."

"I don't know who his new girlfriend is, but I wish it were me," someone else sighed. "I'd go to a hotel with Ben Barrett any night of the week!"

"Well, there you have it," Shanika chirped into the mic. "Scandalous or not, it looks like Ben Barrett has still scandalized the hearts of his female fans."

Scandalized the hearts? What did that even mean?

Sighing, Maggie turned off the television and then nearly fell off the couch when the door to the apartment swung open.

"Oh," she blurted, eyes wide as Ben entered the room. "You're still here?"

"Sure am."

He strode toward her, dropping a set of keys—*her* keys—on the hall table before approaching the living area. He held a large brown paper bag in his hands, and from where she sat, she saw the splotches of grease at the bottom of the bag and the steam rising from the top.

"I went out and got us some Chinese food. I don't like pizza all that much."

"But..."

"You asked me to leave?" He cocked a brow. "That's not going to happen, Mags."

She bristled at his use of her nickname. "And why not?"

"Because you like me. And I happen to like you."

"I also like Joe the hot dog vendor. Doesn't mean I'm going to let him move in with me and turn my life upside down."

"Who said anything about moving in with you?" He flopped down on the couch, set the bag down on the coffee table and shot her a look that said *you don't understand me at all.*

Well, she *didn't* understand him. He was Ben Barrett, for God's sake. After watching that two-minute segment on him, she was pretty sure he could walk out of there and have five phone numbers in his pocket before he even left the building. So why was he sticking around?

"All I want to do is spend a little time with you," he added. "And if you're honest, you'll admit you want to spend time with me." .

"Ben—"

He silenced her by raising his hand, and like an obedient third-grader, her mouth slammed shut.

"I have a proposition for you," he announced.

Wariness circled her insides like a pack of turkey vultures. "What kind of proposition?"

"I'll have sex with you if you let me stay here a while." With a pleasant smile, he began removing items from the take-out bag. He carefully placed each cardboard container on the table, and then reached into the bag for the napkins and cutlery.

She just stared at him. Obviously she'd misheard him, because no way had he just offered to sleep with her in exchange for room and board. Deciding to chalk it up to hallucination, she focused instead on the food he was laying out on the table, wondering what the hell he was doing. She'd told him to check into a hotel, for God's sake, and instead he'd come back with that cocky attitude and a bag of Chinese food that smelled too damn good and made her empty stomach growl in anticipation.

"Gimme that," she sighed, grabbing the carton of egg rolls from his hands.

"That's all you've got to say?" He watched as she munched on a roll, his eyes bewildered. "You're not going to respond to my proposition?"

Damn. She hadn't hallucinated it after all.

But that didn't mean she wanted to discuss it either, so she spared him a withering glance and said, "No."

"Why the fuck not?"

"Because it's so ridiculous it doesn't merit a response."

"It's not ridiculous and you know it."

"What I know," she said, swallowing before reaching for another egg roll, "is that you're nuts. I'm not giving you a place to stay in exchange for sex."

"Why not? We both know you really need the sex."

Her nostrils flared. Deciding it was best to ignore this entire absurd exchange, she reached for a carton of chicken fried rice, grabbed a fork and ate a mouthful of rice. Her silence seemed to work, as Ben closed his mouth, but he continued to watch her, so intently, so knowingly, that it was becoming increasingly difficult to ignore that flicker of heat in her belly.

Fine, so maybe his proposition wasn't totally ridiculous. Maybe the thought of having sex with Ben was even more delicious than this food. Maybe giving him a blow job in the shower had been the most erotic experience of her life and maybe she wanted to do it again.

Didn't mean she'd give in.

"How long is your roommate away for?" Ben finally asked.

"Eight days." She chewed slowly. "Not that it should matter to you. You're not staying here."

He leaned back against the sofa cushions and said, "You don't find my offer the least bit tempting?"

"Nope."

"Liar."

She ignored him and dug into a plate of vegetables, hoping that sooner or later he'd see she was serious and go away.

It was, of course, hoping for too much.

Before she could blink, he'd swiped the fork from her hands and tossed it on the table. Then, without giving her time to protest, he pulled her onto his lap and grasped her hips with his hands so she couldn't move.

"Let me stay with you, Maggie."

"No," she murmured, trying very hard to ignore the warmth of his hands against her hips, the heat of his groin against her thighs.

He dipped his head and brushed a soft kiss over her lips. Her attempt at backing away was futile. He only moved one hand to her head and threaded his fingers through her damp hair, holding her in place.

"Let me stay with you," he whispered into her mouth.

"No."

He licked her lower lip. Captured it with his teeth, nibbling, suckling.

She gave an involuntary moan.

Grinning, Ben pulled back. "C'mon, babe," he said with a teasing note to his sexy voice. "You know you don't want me to leave."

An argument reached her lips, but when she opened her mouth, nothing came out.

"You came to that hotel because you needed a release," he continued. "I can give you that release."

She shifted, trying to ease off his lap, but all she succeeded in doing was rubbing against his crotch, which hardened instantly.

"Forget about Tony. I'll give you all the sex you crave and more."

Her cheeks grew pink and finally she found her voice. "I'm not some virgin you need to deflower."

"I don't want to deflower you. I want to fuck you." His voice took on a seductive tinge. "Eight days. For the next eight days I'll fuck your brains out, Maggie. Anything you want me to do to you, I'll do. Anytime you want it, you'll have it."

Oh God. His words sent bolts of lightning down her spine and straight to her pussy. She'd already come twice today, but suddenly she was aching for release again. How did he manage to do this to her, send her into a state of such mindless lust?

"And all you have to do in return," he finished, "is let me stay here. The way I see it—" his tongue darted out and dragged along her bottom lip, "—you definitely get the better end of the stick, babe."

"You don't play fair," she murmured.

"Like I said, never have." Then he slid his hands underneath her shirt and cupped her braless breasts.

A jolt of pleasure torpedoed into her.

"So, what'll it be, Mags?"

She almost purred as he stroked each breast with his palms and then tweaked her nipples playfully.

"All you've gotta do is give me a place to stay and you have your very own boy toy," he added with an arch of his brows. "You know it's a damn good deal."

It was hard to think with his hands on her tits, but for the life of her, she couldn't shrug them away. They felt too good against her flushed skin, the feel of his hard cock between her legs too damn tantalizing.

"Ground rules," she managed to choke out.

The words surprised her. Ground rules? Was she actually *agreeing* to this?

"Let's hear them," he said with a sigh.

She struggled for breath, gasping when he pinched one nipple with his fingers. Damn him. Didn't he know that by doing that to her he was turning her brain into mush? From the faint grin on his face, he definitely knew.

"You don't interfere with my job," she found herself saying. "And you don't interrupt me when I'm studying."

"Done. Is that it?"

She made a frantic attempt to think of more rules, but none came to mind. Shit. This was way too easy—for him. All he'd had to do was dangle the sex carrot under her nose and she was ready to take a chunk out of it. There should've been a dozen reasons why letting Ben stay with her was a bad, bad idea, but somehow all those reasons eluded her. It didn't help that he was still fondling her breasts and it definitely didn't help that her pussy was so wet, her panties were completely soaked.

And yet the excitement coursing through her gave her pause. Was her roommate right? Was her life so focused on work and school that she'd really lost touch with the rest of the world? Was she really *anti-fun*?

God, she hoped not. She didn't want to be *that woman*. The

one who let her entire life pass her by only to wake up one day and realize she'd missed out.

You have sex twice a year! Of course you're missing out!

She tried to shut out that annoying voice, but it was difficult to ignore the truth. Besides, a few orgasms a year really couldn't be healthy, could it? Didn't her body deserve a week of orgasmic delights? Movie star or not, a hot guy was offering to be her *boy toy*, for fuck's sake. How in her right mind could she turn that down?

"Maggie?" His rough voice broke through her conflicting thoughts.

She glanced down, realizing his hands were still under her shirt, his fingers still caressing her painfully hard nipples and his erection still pressed against her unbelievably wet pussy.

Opening her mouth, she sucked in a breath and said, "Eight days, Barrett. Don't complicate my life."

"And the sex?"

A whisper of a smile tugged at her mouth. "Like you said, anything I want, anytime I want it." She wiggled her lower body into his and added, "Starting now."

Without a word, Ben followed Maggie down the hall, barely able to conceal his smile of satisfaction. He waited while she stepped into the bathroom, then returned with a small box of condoms in her hands. Oh yeah. No question who'd won the battle. Hell, make that the entire fucking war. Not only had he managed to secure himself a place to stay—one out of the prying eyes of the press—he'd convinced Maggie to go to bed with him. Not an easy feat, considering she was obviously a workaholic who viewed sex as a complication.

It still amazed him, how Maggie managed to get by with

only a couple of sexual trysts a year.

Fortunately, he was here to fix that.

They reached her bedroom, and he stood in the doorway for a second, the smile finally reaching his lips when he saw Maggie flop down on the bed and lie on her back. She was wearing a loose cotton tank top and a pair of baggy sweatpants, hardly an outfit that screamed seduction, but something about the casual attire turned him on. He liked that she didn't go to great lengths to doll herself up. The way she dressed reflected that no-nonsense attitude he got from her.

"Come here," she said, her voice both throaty and apprehensive.

He stepped closer, reaching for the hem of his T-shirt then pulling the material over his head. Her eyes widened, just a little, at the sight of his bare chest, and his cock jerked in response. No matter how annoying she claimed to find him, she couldn't deny her attraction and they both knew it.

Unzipping his jeans, he slid them down his legs and kicked them aside.

She raised one delicate brow. "No boxers?"

"I have to go shopping for clothes tomorrow."

"You don't need clothes. You're much more attractive naked."

He held his hand to his heart and shot her a mock smile. "Why, Maggie, was that a compliment?"

"Unfortunately." She released a little sigh. "I should've known better. Your ego's big enough already."

He approached the bed, frowning when she made no move to undress. "Take off your clothes already," he grumbled. "I feel at a disadvantage."

"Take them off for me. You're the boy toy, remember?" She

105

shot him a mischievous grin. "Besides, if you want to stay here, you need to earn the room and board."

He couldn't stop a chuckle. Damn, he liked sassy women. He liked this one in particular, but he suspected that was because she wasn't deliberately trying to be sassy. She simply *was*.

"C'mon, Mr. Movie Star. Let's see what you've got," she taunted.

"Is that a challenge?"

"Yep. And at the moment you're definitely not meeting it."

He sat down on the edge of the bed, his eyes narrowing. "You realize you won't be this smug when I'm through with you?"

Before she could answer, he leaned forward and grasped the waistband of her sweatpants. Very, very slowly, he rolled the material down her smooth legs, brushing his fingertips along every inch of skin that he revealed. He heard her breath hitch and fought a smile. No matter how much she pretended to be in control, he knew that all it would take was one touch, one soft lick to her pussy, and she'd be a moaning, trembling mess again.

He threw the pants on the floor before focusing his attention on her tank top. Instead of removing it though, he simply lowered his head to her chest and kissed her breasts through the shirt. The kiss left a wet spot on the material and caused both her nipples to poke out eagerly.

"Let's get this off," she said, her hands fumbling for the hem of her top.

"No."

He grabbed both her hands with one of his and shoved her wrists over her head, clasping them with his fingers, tightly, so she couldn't move. Dipping his head again, he rubbed his mouth over her covered chest then bit one of her nipples. She flinched, but he knew he hadn't hurt her, the glazed look in her eyes telling him that she most certainly enjoyed the rough way his teeth had captured the rigid bud. He continued to nibble, his tongue pulsing with the need to slide underneath the thin shirt and taste her flesh. But not yet.

Not until she begged for it.

Maybe it made him a pompous ass, but he wanted this woman to beg. She might've agreed to let him stay at her place, might've agreed to hop into bed with him, but her reluctance had been written all over her pretty face. Again she'd acted like she was doing him the favor, and he found himself desperate to prove to her that their attraction went both ways. That she wanted him just as badly as he wanted her.

Still holding her wrists against the headboard, he slid his other hand up her body and cupped one perky breast. He squeezed, hard, enjoying the little whimper of distress she gave. Minute after minute ticked by, but still he made no move to rip off her shirt, instead teasing her breasts and kissing her distended nipples until she squirmed beneath him.

"Please," she finally wheezed out.

He poked his tongue in his cheek and lifted his head to meet her agitated green eyes. "Please what?"

"Please take my shirt off."

"Anything else?" he asked pleasantly.

He saw the cloud of desire and irritation on her face, knew it was hard for her to admit her arousal to him. She surprised him, though. With a strangled groan, she sucked in a long breath then blurted, "Fuck me, Ben. *Please.*"

It was all he needed to hear.

With a groan of his own, he tore the tank top off her body. Literally *tore* it, the thin straps snapping between his fingers. He threw the torn garment aside and pressed his mouth to those delectable tits, feasting on each firm mound. He didn't think he'd ever get his fill, but the heat of her pussy against his groin was too hard to ignore.

Sucking one nipple deep in his mouth, he hooked his thumb under the waistband of her panties and pushed them down. He cupped her, moaning when her juices coated his palm.

"You're so fucking wet," he choked out.

"You seem to make that happen. A lot."

He bristled at her forlorn tone. "Don't act like you don't love how wet I make you."

As if to prove his point, he shoved one finger deep inside her warm, tight cunt and was instantly rewarded with another gush of moisture. His mouth tingled, his tongue suddenly aching with the need to taste this woman again. Releasing her wrists, he planted one last kiss to her breasts and slid down her body until his head was positioned between her thighs.

His tongue traveled along one thigh, licking the smooth skin before dragging toward her clit. Her soft moans drove him wild, lit his entire body on fire, but he managed to hold on to his restraint. He laved her clit with his tongue, continuing to move that one finger in and out of her tight hole.

Maggie gave a breathy whimper as he flicked the tip of his tongue over her swollen bud, and when he began to suck on it, she shuddered, almost violently. He lifted his head, grinning at the sexual heat he saw flashing in her eyes. He skimmed his tongue along her damp labia, adding another finger into the mix and beginning a lazy, sensual rhythm that caused a low moan to escape her lips. Pleased with her reaction, he continued to explore that sweet pussy, enjoying the way she arched her hips to allow him greater access. When he saw her hands clawing at the sheets and heard the desperation lacing her moans, he finally quickened the pace, slid a third finger inside her, and she promptly toppled over the edge.

She came hard, and just listening to her hoarse moans and feeling the erotic tremors that vibrated through her body made his cock twitch with anticipation.

He gave her some time to recover, his head resting on her thigh, his heart pounding like a jackhammer. When he finally felt her orgasm subside, he slid his way up her body, kissed her hard on the mouth and guided his cock to her wet opening. She quickly shifted before he could enter her, wiggling out from under him and pushing him onto his back.

"My turn," she murmured.

"Didn't you just have your turn?" he murmured back.

"Just shut up and enjoy this."

His blood surged as her fingertips grazed his neck, his heart pounding even faster when he noticed the wicked gleam in her eyes. The image of what she'd done to him in the shower, with her mouth, her tongue, her hands, floated into his head and his cock began to ache. He was so turned on he didn't think he could handle another one of her blow jobs, no matter how incredible it was.

"Don't worry, I'll stop before you come," she said in a sexy whisper, as if she'd read his mind.

A second later, her mouth clamped down on his neck. She sucked on his skin, the pressure of her lips causing a shiver to sizzle down his spine and grab hold of his balls. Closing his eyes, he lost himself to sensation, to the feel of Maggie's lips trailing wet kisses along his skin. Her mouth traveled down to his chest, where she nibbled on one flat nipple, then down to his stomach, where she licked the line of hair leading down to his crotch. When she finally reached his cock, he was harder than ever and so close to exploding he could barely move.

One lick, one soft kiss to his pre-come-soaked tip, was all he was willing to allow. Any more and he'd be shooting his load in her mouth, when all he wanted to do was bury his cock inside her wet heat.

Laughing quietly, she put him out of his misery and climbed back up, straddling him with her long legs. "You're close, aren't you, Ben?" She leaned toward the nightstand and reached for one of the condoms in the box she'd placed there.

"What the hell do you think?" he growled. His cock twitched as she covered it with a condom.

Her laugh deepened, a melodic sound that made his erection harden even more, if that was humanly possible. "I expect my boy toys to possess stamina," she said with mock disapproval.

Before he could respond with a comeback, she sucked the breath right out of his lungs by impaling herself onto his dick. White-hot pleasure sliced into him like a knife.

"Still close?" she teased.

He managed a nod, and then lifted his head in an attempt to kiss her.

Like the teasing vixen she was, she shifted her head so his lips connected with her cheek, and then made a tsking sound with her tongue. "None of that," she said. "I'm still having my way with you."

She dipped her head and pressed her mouth to his jaw, planting light, barely-there kisses along his skin. Nibbling on his earlobe, she ground her lower body against his but didn't ride him the way he wanted her to, just rotated her hips slightly. When he made another attempt to kiss her, she allowed it, but this time her tongue was in charge, exploring his mouth with precision.

He groaned, the guttural sound filling the bedroom, and Maggie broke the kiss with a faint grin. "You know," she mused, "I recall you telling me I wouldn't be so smug once you had your way with me...and yet I'm still feeling pretty damn smug."

"Yeah, what about now?"

Without giving her time to react, he dug his fingers into her hips and thrust upwards, driving his cock deeper inside her.

She gasped, her eyes wide with pleasure and surprise. "Now...I'm feeling less smug," she admitted, then cried out when he gave another hard thrust.

"And now?"

"Now...I'm...oh God..." Her eyes had glazed over and she looked like she was struggling to speak.

He lifted his hips off the bed again.

"And now?"

She gave a breathy moan. "Now I just want to fuck you."

And she did. She rode him so hard he could barely see straight, her pussy clamped so tightly over his dick he was almost in pain from the pleasure swirling inside him.

He locked her gaze with his and watched as her expression changed from aroused to blissful, and then she was coming again, her inner muscles squeezing his cock and triggering a climax so intense his vision became hazy.

With one last shudder, the wave crashed and subsided, leaving them limp. Maggie collapsed on top of him, her breasts crushed against his damp chest, her breathing ragged.

After a moment she moved off him and lay flat on her back, her gorgeous breasts rising and falling with each breath. He stayed quiet, trying to control his own breathing, trying to recover from the body-numbing orgasm that had just crashed into him like a hurricane.

"So anytime I want it?" she finally murmured.

He found himself laughing again. "That's what I promised, didn't I?"

"Good." She rolled over, pressed her face against his chest and promptly fell asleep in his arms.

Chapter Seven

"You look strange," Trisha said matter-of-factly when Maggie walked into the Olive the next evening.

Feeling her cheeks grow warm, Maggie met her friend's curious gaze. "Strange?"

"Yeah. Are you sick? You're kinda flushed."

It didn't surprise her that she looked flushed. She *felt* flushed. Before she'd left the apartment to come to work, Ben had worked his magic on her again, once with that wicked tongue of his, the second time with that thick cock she couldn't seem to get enough of. For a moment she was tempted to tell Trisha all about it, but quickly quelled that urge. If Trisha found out she was currently shacked up with a movie star, the entire world would know about it in a matter of minutes.

So all she said was, "Maybe I'm getting sick."

Her co-worker looked her up and down, those eerily-perceptive brown eyes piercing into her. Finally, Trisha gave a brisk nod. "You had sex."

The flush returned to her cheeks. "What? Of course not."

"Liar. You had sex. It's written all over your face." Trisha's eyes lit up. "Tony's still in town?"

Since it was the perfect out, she quickly nodded in confirmation. "Yep. Still here."

"Well?"

"Well what?"

"I want details! You obviously got laid last night. I, on the other hand, went to a high school basketball game with Lou. I can't even remember the last time I had an orgasm, so I really need to live vicariously through you."

Fortunately their manager walked over and put an end to the conversation before she could answer. *Un*fortunately, Linda's brisk strides and the frown on her face told Maggie that her manager wasn't happy.

"Trisha, tend to your tables," Linda said in lieu of greeting.

Looking puzzled by the older woman's harsh tone, Trisha simply nodded and hurried away.

Linda turned to Maggie. "I need to speak with you."

She was feeling a little puzzled herself. Straightening out the bottom of her apron, she leaned awkwardly against the counter and shot her boss a quizzical look. "What's up?"

"A complaint was made about you."

"What?"

"A customer filed a complaint after you left on Saturday." Linda's frown deepened. "Apparently you were ridiculing his drink order. He was very unhappy with your behavior."

Ridiculing a drink order?

She ran over Saturday night's events in her mind, trying to remember everyone she'd served. She didn't recall being particularly rude to anyone. It wasn't her style to be rude and she honestly couldn't think of what she might have said to warrant a complaint.

Obviously sensing her bewilderment, Linda added, "The customer said he felt you were belittling his masculinity."

Oh. *Oh.* The memory of Wayne the daiquiri man entered

her brain. She'd been thinking about Ben at the time, distracted by the fact that he was waiting outside for her and demanding to stay at her apartment, but she'd apologized for the remark, hadn't she? No, of course she'd apologized. Evidently the customer hadn't been satisfied with that.

"I wasn't belittling him," she said in her defense. "I was distracted and said something—to myself. I explained to him that I wasn't referring to him or his drink."

"Regardless, he was unhappy, and unhappy customers are bad for business. I know you've been busy with your school work, Maggie, but try to stay focused when you're here at the Olive. I'm not going to put the complaint in your file, but I just want you to be aware of it."

"All right. Um, thanks for letting me know." She played with the tie of her apron, adding, "It won't happen again, Linda."

"Good. Don't forget, Jeremy will be here next week, so everyone needs to be on top of their game. Best behavior, okay? Don't antagonize customers."

She wanted to protest that she hadn't antagonized anyone, but Linda was already walking away.

With a small sigh, she grabbed her tray and headed for the couple who'd just seated themselves at one of her tables. She pasted a smile on her face and diligently took their order, all the while thinking about how she couldn't wait to get home. Ben Barrett might be a movie star, not to mention a huge headache, but he was damn good in bed. And right now, she could really use another orgasm. Or two. Or ten.

It only took three days for Ben to realize that Maggie Reilly needed a lot more than sex. She needed a goddamn vacation.

He honestly couldn't understand how she lived the way she did. Her life revolved around work and school, and her self-discipline was almost mind-boggling. She spent the mornings studying and writing papers, and the afternoons at the community center where she volunteered. Then she came home and buried her nose in a textbook for a couple more hours. By the evening, she was getting ready to go to work, where she spent the night waiting tables. She returned around two a.m. and went straight to bed. She ate only when he forced her to, and shot down his suggestions that she take a walk or watch some television with him. In fact, the only time she actually seemed grateful for his company was when they were in bed together.

It almost made him feel slutty—that she seemed more interested in his body than in his attempts for them to get to know each other. Not that he was complaining about the sex. If anything, the sex only got better each time they got naked.

But it seriously bothered him, the way Maggie didn't make any time for herself. He didn't think the words *relax* or *unwind* were even in her vocabulary. And he was growing more and more distressed each time he found her asleep at the computer desk and had to carry her back to bed at four in the morning.

Not that he didn't appreciate a solid work ethic, because he did. Despite what Maggie thought, he worked hard for the money sitting in his bank account, the money he'd earned before Gretchen had shocked him and the world by leaving him a part of her fortune. Acting wasn't all fun and games, and when he was in the middle of an intense shoot, Ben didn't even leave his house.

Still, he always took breaks, always made sure his work didn't monopolize his life. He'd seen a fair amount of actors crash and burn, make six films back to back and get so lost in the work they didn't even know who they were anymore.

Maggie might not be in the movie industry, but she was a workaholic through and through. She needed to slow down and unwind, and he'd officially dubbed himself the man who'd help her do that.

It was time to step in. He'd promised her he wouldn't complicate her life, but this was just plain ridiculous. Sure, he loved having a quiet place to hide out, but how much longer could he really watch Maggie waste her life away?

At the moment, she was sitting on the other end of the couch, devouring a book about autism, and she hadn't gotten up in three hours. He wanted to suggest they order a pizza or something, but he knew trying to get her to quit when she was still absorbed in her work would get him nowhere.

Instead, he flicked on the television, instantly groaning when he saw what was on.

For the first time all afternoon, Maggie glanced up from her book. Her gaze followed his and rested on the screen. She made a face when she saw the entertainment show. "Don't these people have lives?" she grumbled.

He ignored her and turned up the volume.

"Ben Barrett's newest flame must be keeping him very busy," the host said with a mischievous grin. "The sexy bad boy has been off the radar for nearly a week now and everyone is wondering how he's been spending his time..."

"Should we tell them?" Maggie said with a tiny grin.

"Was that an honest-to-God joke?" he returned with mock-amazement. "I didn't think you were capable of anything but working."

"Ha ha."

"Early in the week, Barrett's car was found vandalized in front of a New York City strip club," the host continued. "It was later revealed he had spent the night in a hotel with an unidentified woman..."

"They make you sound like a sleazebag," Maggie said, rolling her eyes.

"Although rumors are swirling that Barrett is out of sight due to an impromptu elopement with his mysterious new lady—"

Maggie burst out laughing.

"—a source close to the actor admits that Barrett is keeping a low profile because of the Gretchen Goodrich scandal. Goodrich, who was the wife of Oscar-winning director Alan Goodrich, recently left Barrett a sizable fortune after—"

Ben turned off the television with an angry frown. Damn vultures. Why the fuck couldn't they just leave him alone? Why couldn't they let Gretchen rest in peace?

"So..." Maggie's quiet voice broke through his troubled thoughts. "Are you ever going to tell me about what happened with Gretchen Goodrich?"

"Sure." He turned his head and stared her down. "If you agree to take a damn break for a couple of days."

"I don't take breaks."

"Then start."

Annoyance flickered in her emerald eyes. "We've been through this already."

"And I still don't think it's healthy, the way you bury yourself in work and school."

"It doesn't matter what you think. It's my life, Ben."

"Yeah. Sure. It's your life." He rose to his feet, unable to stop the scowl from creasing his mouth. "I'm taking a shower. I'd ask you to join me but you've still got, what, three hundred more pages to read?" He stared pointedly at the textbook in her

118

lap before walking out of the living room.

She didn't follow him, and he hadn't expected her to. The past three days had taught him that Maggie shut down the moment he criticized her lifestyle.

He strode into the bathroom and ripped off his T-shirt and jeans, then turned on the water and stepped into the shower stall. As the warm water slid down his body, he dunked his head under the spray and released a low groan. Why was he letting Maggie's workaholic ways get to him anyway? The television segment he'd just seen confirmed that the media storm surrounding him was still going strong, which meant he definitely needed to stay out of sight for a while longer. That's what he'd wanted, a place to hide out for a while, and he was getting that from Maggie. He was also getting some pretty incredible sex, which was just another perk.

Yet it pissed him off, the way Maggie drove herself to the point of exhaustion. He liked her—fuck, he liked her a lot. And what he *didn't* like was seeing someone he liked wasting her life away. He didn't know what made her do it, why she felt she had to work so freaking hard, but he did know he wanted to help her.

But how the hell could he ever break down Maggie's impenetrable devotion to her job and her annoying tendency to choose responsibility over fun?

He stood in the stall for a moment, letting the water course down his body, and then the answer came to him.

With a sly grin, he shut off the water and stepped onto the fluffy pink mat outside the shower stall. Grabbing a towel, he wrapped it around his waist and left the bathroom, heading for Maggie's bedroom. He sat at the edge of the bed and picked up the phone from its cradle. Glancing over to make sure he'd closed the door, he punched the number for information. A few seconds later, he got what he was looking for and dialed another number.

"The Olive Martini. Trisha here."

"Why hello, Trisha." He lowered his voice, looked once again at the door, and then said, "I'm calling about Maggie Reilly."

"Who is this?" The voice on the other end thickened with suspicion.

He faltered for a moment before responding with, "It's Tony."

"Tony? Oh my God! I didn't recognize your voice."

Shit. He hadn't banked on any of the other wait staff knowing the infamous Tony.

"Uh, I'm trying to speak quietly. Maggie's in the other room and I don't want her to overhear."

"Gotcha. So what's up?"

"Well, I need you to do me a really big favor..."

"I want to take you on a trip."

Maggie's head shot up, not so much from Ben's sudden reappearance but more from the words that exited his sexy mouth. He approached the couch, clad in a pair of jeans and a navy-blue long-sleeved shirt, his hair still damp from the shower. His jaw was tight and his mouth was set in a very firm line, as if he'd come out here expecting a fight and prepared to win it.

His words hung in the air. A trip? Hadn't he listened to a word she'd said ten minutes ago?

"I don't have time to take—"

"I'm not talking a week-long vacation," he interrupted,

catching the disbelief in her eyes. "I'm talking one night. Well, two, since we'd leave tonight and come back Saturday morning."

"I'm working tomorrow, Ben."

"So call in sick." He offered a small shrug. "C'mon, babe, it's just one day."

Her jaw tensed at his flippant tone. "I can't lie to my manager."

"Maggie."

"Ben."

She didn't like the way he was looking at her, with that secretive little smile that said he was up to something. But how could he be? He couldn't force her to go away with him. Couldn't tie her up and drag her out of the city.

Before she could further analyze that sly expression on his face, the phone rang. Grateful for the interruption, she leaned over and plucked the cordless from its cradle, noting the blinking red light on the answering machine that indicated there was a new message. She'd forgotten that she'd turned the ringer off earlier, after three irritating telemarketers had called one after the other.

"Hello?" She avoided eye contact with Ben as she pressed the phone to her ear.

"Hey, it's me."

Since Trisha rarely ever called her, Maggie's guard instantly shot up a few feet. She didn't know where that suspicious tug at her gut came from, but she couldn't ignore that *something-is-fishy* feeling.

"What's up, Trish?"

"I need you to switch shifts with me. I'll work for you tomorrow night if you do Saturday."

Something was fishy, all right.

Her head swiveled in Ben's direction, but he seemed completely uninterested in her conversation, and oblivious to its content.

Of course, he also happened to be an actor, so what he seemed to be wasn't all that reliable.

"Why can't you work Saturday?" she asked, eyes narrowed.

"You won't even believe it."

"Try me."

"Lou's taking me to see a Broadway show," Trisha replied in a bubbly voice. "And it was *his* idea. Isn't that amazing?"

"What show?"

"Huh?"

"What show is he taking you to see?"

"*The Puppeteer.*"

If she'd caught Trisha in a lie, she had no freaking clue. Her ignorance about Broadway musicals, not to mention most pop culture, was definitely the proverbial thorn in her side. She'd have to check it on the 'Net later. As it was, she found it hard to believe that Trisha would magically want to cover her shift two minutes after Ben announced his plan to take her on a trip.

"So will you do it, Mags?"

"Uh..."

"Please say yes," Trisha begged. "You know how much I complain about Lou never paying attention to me. You've *got* to let me have this."

A sigh lodged in the back of her throat. Damn it. The guilt card worked every time.

"Sure, of course I'll take your shift."

"Great! I owe you a million!"

You sure do, Maggie thought ruefully as she hung up the phone and turned her attention back to Ben. He'd moved across the room and now stood in front of the television, oddly fascinated by the Cary Grant photos Summer's grandmother had mounted on the wall.

"Apparently I now have the day off tomorrow."

He turned around, his features revealing nothing. "Looks like fate decided to step in."

"Fate," she repeated, unable to stop that mistrustful cloud swirling in the forefront of her brain.

"So does this mean the trip is on?"

She took great pleasure in bursting that balloon of hope floating around in his gaze. "Nope."

Pop. The balloon dissolved into an annoyed glimmer. "Why the hell not?"

"I volunteer four days a week, in the afternoons. Fridays and Saturdays are two of those days. It's a requirement for my college program."

His broad shoulders sagged with disappointment. He looked really cute when he was dejected, but Maggie refused to let that puppy-dog gaze get to her. In fact, this was a conversation she'd had so many times, it was almost soothing. The men in her life made demands, her schedule got in the way, and they left in a huff. It was a routine now, and the one thing she always gained the most comfort from was her routine.

She softened her tone. "You could still take that trip to...wherever it is you wanted us to go."

"I guess you'll never know," he muttered. For the first time since she'd met him, he'd lost that confident aura.

The annoying blinking light on the answering machine

flashed in the corner of her eye. "Hold on. You can continue being mad at me in a second," she teased.

She pressed the play button and a familiar female voice filled the room. "Maggie, it's Gloria. I really hope you get this message before you show up for your shift tomorrow."

Gloria Rodriguez was the facilitator of the Broger Center, and the second Maggie heard her soft Hispanic voice an uneasy feeling climbed up her throat.

"Libby Martin, you know, the little girl with the freckles? Well, she's come down with the chicken pox. I know you haven't had any contact with her lately, but some of the other kids have and they're showing symptoms too. So if you've never had the chicken pox, I'd advise that you don't come in tomorrow."

Damn you, Fate.

"Actually, don't come for at least a week, just to be safe. The infectious period is about five days, but chicken pox could be dangerous for adults. So stay away if you've never had it, kiddo. Call me to let me know."

Maggie listened to the soft click, then the automated voice announced she had no other messages.

"So...just for my own curiosity," Ben began, his husky voice coming out in a soft drawl, "have you ever had the chicken pox, sweetheart?"

She made an inaudible noise, and then set her jaw so tight her teeth hurt.

"What was that?" he prompted. "I couldn't make out your answer."

She slowly opened her mouth, relaxing her muscles with a long, calming breath. "No, Ben, I can't say I've ever had the chicken pox."

He made a clucking noise with his tongue. "What a shame."

She met his gaze and saw the amusement dancing around in those striking blue eyes. "I'm sure *Fate* would agree with you."

His lips twitched. "So how long will it take you to pack?"

Chapter Eight

Whoever said fate was a cruel mistress had no idea what they were talking about, because apparently fate was very much on Ben's side. He may have gone behind Maggie's back to get her out of work, but he'd totally forgotten about her volunteer work. Fortunately, fate stepped in after she'd dropped that I-volunteer-four-days-a-week bomb in his lap. Okay, well, maybe not fate exactly, but an itchy childhood ailment that had irritated him immensely when he was six years old.

Gotta love the chicken pox.

He was actually surprised Maggie hadn't put up more of a fight after her tidy little schedule shot up in flames. He'd expected her to, but she'd yet again impressed him with her graceful admission of defeat.

Instead of hurling more excuses at him, she'd calmly walked into her bedroom and packed an overnight bag, and now they were seated in the back of a cab headed to the airport. Much to Ben's delight, he had two whole nights to make her realize he was exactly what she needed.

Call him arrogant, call him a presumptuous ass, but he'd spent enough time with Maggie Reilly to know the woman needed a wake-up call.

From him.

Who are you really helping here?

Ben bit the inside of his cheek, momentarily startled by the little accusation in his head.

Maggie. He was helping Maggie, right?

Or was he starting to feed on the way Maggie made him forget about his mess of a life?

He'd never been one to duck and hide when troubles arose, but these past few days with Maggie reminded him of what life before fame had been like. It brought back memories of growing up in Ohio, of being able to take a girl out without it winding up in the tabloids, of being able to sing along to the Beach Boys without a sound bite popping up on the Internet. And damn it, he wanted to hold on to that unburdened feeling for as long as he could, to think about someone other than himself for a while. He didn't know where it was all heading, but for the moment he needed to be around her. Needed that feeling of being a regular person.

And he *would* be helping her. He'd told her he'd give her all the sex she wanted, and he'd done that, but it was becoming unsettlingly obvious that Maggie needed more than sex. She needed fun. Relaxation. A *life*.

"Where exactly are we going?" she asked, jarring him from his thoughts.

"It's a surprise."

"Did I mention I don't like surprises?"

"No, and mentioning it now won't get you any answers." He reached over and squeezed her lower thigh, then tried to ignore the jolt of desire in his groin. "Trust me, you'll like it."

She had better like it. Ben had pulled so many strings he could officially put the New York Philharmonic out of business. If Maggie didn't appreciate what he was doing for her, he'd owe a few big names some big favors.

After the cab driver dropped them off at the International terminal at La Guardia airport, Ben helped Maggie out of the taxi and slung her overnight bag over his shoulder. "Ready?"

"How can I be ready when I don't know what to be ready for?"

He grinned and pulled the rim of his Yankees cap low to his forehead. Where they were going, he probably wouldn't get recognized, but better safe than sorry, his mom always said.

They were met at the end of the taxi stand by an airport employee, who ushered them onto a small private shuttle. As they drove away from the terminal, Maggie shot him a puzzled look.

"Seriously, where are we going?" she repeated.

"Be patient, Red."

She made a little irritated sound and closed her mouth. A few minutes later, they pulled up in front of a large private hangar, its doors open to reveal a white and gold Gulfstream IV. Sexiest jet ever built, in Ben's opinion.

Maggie's eyes were two green saucers as she stared at the sleek plane. "Please don't tell me this is yours."

"I'm not that rich," he replied in a mild tone.

As they followed their airport guide out of the shuttle, Maggie couldn't take her eyes off the plane. Whether or not Ben owned it suddenly became a moot point. That he knew someone who did was enough to leave her wide-eyed and speechless.

People actually lived like this? She'd always known it, but seeing it was an entirely different matter altogether. Seeing it also brought a tiny spark of resentment to her gut. She had nothing against someone who could afford his own private jet, but it was just a reminder of everything she didn't have. Not that she aspired to be a jet-setting billionaire who went through hundred dollar bills like Tic Tacs, but it would be nice not to worry about saving her pennies to pay for basic essentials.

The person who owned this plane probably only worried about when it would be time to trade in for a newer model.

As Ben exchanged a few words with the pilot, who'd stepped out of the cabin at their arrival, Maggie swept her gaze along the length of the jet. In gold lettering, scrawled across the side, were the words "Papa G".

Jeez, did this monstrosity belong to a *mobster*?

She seriously hoped not.

"We're good to go," Ben told her, shifting her overnight back to his left shoulder so he could put his arm around her again.

She managed a nod and followed him up the steps leading into the cabin. Inside, she openly gaped at the surroundings. There were about twelve seats in the cabin, white leather, with gold seatbelts that—God, those couldn't be *real* diamonds studded along the buckles. Instead of a tray that folded out of the back of each seat, each pair of chairs faced another, and bolted onto the floor between them were honest-to-God *poker* tables. With green felt and everything.

"Who owns this?" she blurted out.

Ben shot her a tiny little grin. "Papa G."

"*Who*?"

"Papa G." He furrowed his brows. "You know, the rapper?"

Her expression remained blank, causing Ben to sigh.

"You honestly don't know who Papa G is? LA gangsta rap, came out last year with the hit single 'Where's my Bling, Bitch?'"

She'd entered the Twilight Zone. Only thing missing was the creepy music and a guy named Mulder...or was that a different show?

"So you're borrowing this plane from a rapper who sings about bitches?" she said slowly.

"He doesn't sing, he raps. And yes, I'm borrowing his jet. Papa made a cameo in one of my films last year, so I called in a favor."

"Oh."

There was really nothing more to say, except maybe inquire as to what bling was, but she didn't feel like making an idiot out of herself in front of Ben and the stone-faced pilot lurking near the cockpit entrance.

"The flight plan has been filed, and we're all fueled," the pilot said in a professional voice. "If you could take your seats and strap in, we'll be ready for take-off." He disappeared into the cockpit and closed the door.

Ben gestured to one of the window seats. "It's all yours."

She gulped. "No, it's okay, you take it."

"You sure?"

"Uh-huh."

During her gawking of G Pappy's plane, she seemed to have forgotten one very important, very terrifying thought—she'd never flown before.

Her knees knocked together as she sank into one of the leather chairs and fumbled with the seatbelt. Although the temperature in the cabin was cool, her entire body grew hot. Her nerves scampered around like an anxious kitten.

Fanning her scorching cheeks with one hand, she tried to assume a calm expression, and then turned to Ben and asked, "How familiar are you with the current plane crash statistics?"

"Huh?"

"Plane crashes." She gulped a few times, trying to bring

some saliva back into her arid mouth. "How often do they occur? Are smaller planes more likely to go down than larger ones?"

Ben's movie star mouth stretched out in an amazed smile. "Oh man. You're scared of flying, aren't you?"

"What? No. I mean, I don't know. I've never flown before, so I'm not sure if I'm scared of flying."

A soft laugh rolled out of his chest. "It'll be fine, babe. You're more likely to get hit by a bus than die in a plane crash. That's a fact."

His reply only mollified her slightly, and her nerves continued gnawing at her stomach, especially when the jet lurched forward and started wheeling out of the hangar. It rolled toward one of the runways and a second later the pilot's voice crackled over the loudspeaker to announce their take-off.

Maggie kept her gaze on her lap as the plane sped down the long strip. Her stomach turned as the wheels lifted off the runway. You have a better chance of getting hit by a bus, she told herself, and then repeated the mantra in her head as the jet made its ascent.

"Just take a quick peek," Ben urged. He placed a hand on her chin in an attempt to direct her gaze to the window. "Look how gorgeous the city looks from the air."

Curiosity got the best of her. She leaned across Ben's chest and pressed her nose to the square plastic window, then gasped. "Wow, you're right."

The plane continued to climb into the sky, providing a beautiful view of the cityscape below. Though the sun hadn't quite set entirely, the lights of Manhattan sparkled up at them, the high-rises and skyscrapers growing smaller and smaller the higher they went. She squinted and noticed how tiny the cars speeding across the George Washington Bridge looked, like the miniature toy cars one of her foster brothers used to play with.

Everything looked pretty and surreal, and for the first time all day, a genuine smile reached her lips.

The smile soon faltered, however, when she realized she was draped across Ben's chest. That her breasts were squashed into one of his muscular arms. Awareness prickled her skin, seared right through her sweater and made her nipples pebble against her thin bra. She knew he felt those tight buds, because he slowly moved his arm so that the sleeve of his leather jacket rubbed against her.

What was the matter with her? How was it possible that she *still* hadn't gotten enough of this man? He'd been staying at her apartment for five days, for God's sake. They'd already had sex more times than she could count. So how come every time she looked at him, every time he looked at her, the desire was as fierce and as potent as it had been that first night at the hotel?

"It's a great view, isn't it?" he murmured.

She turned to see his blue eyes glued to her mouth and almost licked her lips in anticipation of his kiss. It embarrassed her, how badly she wanted this man. She should be angry with him for whisking her away when she still had so much work to do and instead all she could think about was ripping his clothes off.

"Crimson red."

She shot him a look. "What?"

"Crimson red," he repeated. "The color of your cheeks. You're embarrassed."

"You know how I'm feeling from my cheeks?"

"Yep." He shrugged. "A big part of acting is reading other people's expressions. That way you know how to react."

A tiny ringing sound filled the jet, indicating they could unbuckle their seatbelts, which they both did.

She crossed her legs and gave him a thoughtful look. "I keep forgetting you're an actor. You definitely don't fit my idea of a celebrity. Though you do fill the arrogance criteria to a T, by the way."

He grinned. "It's part of my natural charm."

"Keep telling yourself that."

"You know," he added, his features growing serious, "it's really easy to fall into the Hollywood trap once you become famous. You could be the most down-to-earth, kind-hearted person and then you get to Hollywood and your ego inflates like a helium balloon. Suddenly you're stepping over people to get ahead, or drowning in a lifestyle that has the power to kill you. Sex, drugs and rock 'n roll, that sort of thing."

"So how'd you escape the trap?"

"I have a very good mother." He shifted over so they were face to face, and something really wholesome and genuine flickered in his gorgeous eyes. "She always made sure I had a good head on my shoulders, even if it meant slapping it into place."

Envy gripped at her, but she tried to look casual. It wasn't Ben's fault she hadn't lucked out in the maternal role model department, or that her voice would never contain that tinge of love and admiration when she spoke of her own mother.

"What about your father?" she asked.

"He ran off with another woman when I was two. Haven't seen him since."

She offered a bitter smile. "Join the club."

"Your dad took off too?"

"My dad wasn't even in the picture to begin with. My

mother was the one who did the running." She swallowed. "I grew up in foster care."

"Did you always live in New York?"

"Yep. Did you always live in Hollywood?"

"God, no. Do you think I'd be this normal if I had? Actually, I grew up in Cobb Valley, Ohio, a town with a population of, oh, about two thousand."

"Seriously?"

"Seriously. Most of my classes in high school had about ten kids total." He laughed. "And down the street from my house there was a drugstore with an honest-to-God malt shop in the back. I'm not making this up."

Hearing Ben talk about his hometown brought on two reactions. First, it warmed her heart, probably because it amazed her that the movie star she'd spent the night Googling could talk so unpretentiously about his roots. The second reaction was discomfort, which was harder to decipher.

Being attracted to him was one thing, but getting to know him? Learning about his childhood and chuckling about the malt shop down the street? Telling him about her dismal upbringing? It was too...intimate.

Figure that one out. They'd seen each other naked, but it was the swapping of life stories she found intimate?

"Can I get you anything to drink?"

Maggie nearly fell out of her seat at the sound of the sugar-sweet female voice. She hadn't thought there was anybody else on board aside from the pilot, and the sudden appearance of a petite blonde in a stewardess uniform made her wonder who else was hiding in the back of the jet. G Pappy himself?

"I'll take coffee." Ben glanced over at her. "Do you want anything, babe?"

Did the flight attendant know who Ben was? Probably. And he'd just *babed* her, right there in front of the woman! Great. She probably thought Maggie was his latest piece of arm candy.

"I want...to use the washroom," she blurted, knowing her cheeks had turned crimson all over again.

This entire situation was too surreal for her. The private jet, the movie star, the fact that she was really starting to *like* the movie star.

Again, way too intimate.

She scurried out of her seat and gave the stewardess a fake smile before hurrying toward the lavatory sign at the end of the aisle.

Inside the surprisingly roomy washroom, she flopped down on the closed toilet seat—also a gaudy gold color—and raked both hands through her hair. God, this was so unlike her. How could she have just shoved all her responsibilities aside and agreed to this silly trip? Yeah, she had the day off from work tomorrow and the week-long chicken-pox-induced vacation from the community center, but think of all the homework she could've gotten out of the way.

Instead, she'd allowed Ben to whisk her away to...to where? She still had no clue where they were going, and that only made her stomach bubble with annoyance. She wasn't cut out for life without plans and schedules, for spur-of-the-moment decisions and movie stars who made her heartbeat race.

She'd seen all those pictures on the web. Ben with a Brazilian supermodel. Ben with a gorgeous soap star. Ben at the Golden Globes. Ben on *The Oprah Winfrey Show*.

The man was a star. A hot, womanizing star. He had the looks and the money to make any woman with a pulse drool at his feet, so why was he hanging around with a waitress from Manhattan?

It couldn't be the thrill of the chase, because truth be told, he'd already caught her. He'd already broken down her defenses by luring her on this mysterious vacation.

What more could he possibly want?

Before she could attempt to come up with an answer, the door handle clicked and Ben strolled in, oblivious to the stunned look on her face.

She stumbled to her feet. "What are you doing in here? What if I was peeing?"

"You weren't," he replied with a shrug. "What you *were* doing was taking too long, and I figured you were scheming to find a way to ditch me when we land."

"I wasn't scheming. I was musing."

"About me?"

"No." The lie filled the lavatory, but before Ben could call her on it, she curled her fingers over her hips and donned her best I-mean-business expression. "We need to get a few things straight."

"Oh, do we?"

He stepped closer, and suddenly the bathroom wasn't as roomy as she'd thought. It was tiny. Oppressive. So tiny and oppressive that Ben's big sexy body was about two inches away from hers, that his stubble-covered chin hovered over her forehead and his warm breath heated the top of her head. Oh, and that the growing tent in his pants would soon poke against her belly.

It was too tempting, being in an enclosed space with this man.

Being anywhere near him, for that matter.

"We need to set boundaries," she managed to say despite her Sahara-dry throat.

He licked his bottom lip. "I don't like boundaries, Red."

"I'm sure you don't, but we still need some. I need to know you'll keep your end of the bargain."

"I don't remember any bargains being made."

His voice grew rough as he eliminated another inch between them. Now his erection pressed against her navel, empirically proving that belly buttons could indeed get turned on.

"I promised you a place to stay. For eight days," she added firmly. "I want you to promise that when the time is up, you'll…"

"I'll what? I'll leave?"

"Y-yes."

He snaked one hand up her back, cradled her head and tilted it so they were eye-to-eye. With his other hand, he wedged her flush against the wall, and then shoved one denim-clad leg between her thighs.

There was something seriously kinky about the way he'd so efficiently trapped her in place. He could have his way with her right this second, screw her standing up in the bathroom of a rapper's private jet, and there was nothing she'd be able to do except hang on for the ride.

The naughty scenario caused a drop of moisture to pool inside her panties, and she knew Ben could feel the heat emanating from her core.

"You're ruining the mood," he murmured, tightening his grip on her waist.

"How am I doing that?"

"You're talking about us parting ways."

"Just promise me we'll say goodbye when the eight days are up." She forced out the words, if only to appease her own peace of mind.

"I'll promise later." He wiggled his leg and the friction it made over her fleece pants drove her mad.

"Ben, please, just promise. I told you, I don't want any complications in my life. You're the boy toy, remember?" God, it was getting harder to formulate words when he kept rubbing his thigh against her like that.

"Fine." He slanted his head and offered a placating smile. "I promise not to complicate your life."

It wasn't the guarantee she'd asked for, but with her clit swollen from his hard muscular thigh rubbing against it and her nipples so hard they actually hurt, suddenly the last thing she wanted to do was talk.

"Ever done it on an airplane?" His voice was husky, silky as a caress, and thick with sexual promise.

"Can't say I have."

She gasped as he tugged at the waistband of her pants and slid them down, along with her underwear. Fleece and cotton pooled around her ankles, leaving her exposed from the waist down.

"Well, now you can."

She waited for him to unzip his jeans and thrust that rock-hard erection inside her, but he didn't. Instead, he stretched one arm in the direction of the pristine white sink and fumbled with the drawer beneath it. A second later he held up a handful of brightly colored condom packets.

"Choose your poison," he teased.

She cupped him over the denim and gave his hard ridge a squeeze. "I choose this one."

He choked out a laugh and shot her a look so full of hunger and lust she almost came on the spot. Those metallic blue eyes swept from her flushed face to her slick folds, devouring her body in a way that made her knees thump together.

Oh sweet lord. She'd already experienced so much with this man. His hands. His mouth. His tongue.

And it still wasn't enough.

With an impatient growl, she snatched one of the condoms from his hand, tore open the package and reached for his zipper. He laughed again, but she didn't care. She couldn't take it anymore. She simply couldn't.

She freed him from his jeans and rolled the latex down his smooth, throbbing cock.

"I need you inside," she ordered. "Now."

"Yes, ma'am."

He planted one hand on her ass and angled her body for better access, then closed his mouth over hers. Before she could blink, he slid into her pussy with a thrust so hard she wasn't surprised when the plane actually shook.

Wait a second—the plane *shook*?

A light knock rapped against the lavatory door. "Mr. Barrett?" came the flight attendant's voice.

Ben let out a string of curses so utterly indecent Maggie's cheeks grew warm. "You've got to be kidding me," he muttered.

His erection continued to throb inside her, and her inner muscles involuntarily tightened over him, causing him to swear again. He gripped her waist to keep her from moving.

"What is it?" he called through the closed door.

"I'm sorry to bother you, but the captain just announced we're experiencing some turbulence. It's very light, but you and your guest will need to return to your seats."

Ben mumbled something under his breath.

"What'd you say?" she whispered.

"I said fuck."

"Oh."

His lips curved with amusement. "You've really got to stop answering everything with 'oh'."

He started to withdraw, but she held his hips in place. "She said light turbulence, right?"

One of his dark brows shot upwards. "She did say light."

Maggie's mouth lifted in a little grin. "I can be fast. What about you?"

"I too can be fast."

She choked back a laugh, and then gasped as he drove into her again. She gripped his taut ass, arched her hips to meet his hurried thrusts, and slid her hand down to stimulate her clit. Not that she needed much stimulation. She came so quickly and so hard that she shocked herself, and she had to clamp her lips together to stop from crying out. Slamming into her with abandon, Ben climaxed a moment later, groaning softly in her ear and palming her breasts over her sweater.

They stood there for a few seconds, breathing heavily, until he finally pulled out and disposed of the condom.

"We should return to our seats," he said, lips twitching with silent laughter.

A tiny smile tugged at her mouth. "Right."

Then she pulled up her pants, smoothed her hair with her hands, and followed Ben out of G Pappy's bathroom. As they nonchalantly strolled past the expressionless stewardess, Maggie tried very, very hard to act as if doing the nasty in a private jet lavatory was absolutely nothing to be embarrassed about.

Chapter Nine

"I can't believe we're in the Bahamas," Maggie breathed as they walked through the airport terminal a couple of hours later.

Ben struggled to keep up with her energized strides. He practically chased her across Lynden Pindling International Airport toward the exit, a difficult task considering his cock still throbbed from the mind-blowing sex they'd had just an hour ago.

"C'mon, Ben, you're slacking here," Maggie chided, already out the door before he could reply.

He stepped outside. A humid breeze instantly swept over him and made his T-shirt stick to his chest. Damn, he seriously hoped the hotel manager had remembered his request for a change of clothes.

"Tony has told me so much about the Bahamas, but I never thought I'd get to see it for myself," Maggie remarked.

A muscle twitched in his jaw. "New rule—you're not allowed to mention Two-Time Tony while you're with me."

She cocked her head, causing strands of red hair to fall onto her forehead. "Two-Time?"

"You know, because he only comes two times a year. Literally."

To his surprise, Maggie let out a husky laugh. Well. Maybe he should've whisked her away from the city sooner. The island air seemed to lighten her up.

"So, what now?" She stared at the crowd of travelers bustling around and the taxi drivers loading suitcases into the trunks of their cabs.

"Now, we get into that car right over there—" he pointed to the black Lincoln at the end of a long line of cars, "—and we start our trip."

Maggie grinned. "Sounds like a plan."

A moment later they were in the backseat of the Lincoln, speeding into Nassau toward the marina, where a boat would be waiting for them. The sun began to set just as they reached the marina, dipping toward the horizon and filling the sky with shades of pink and orange. Ben hid a smile as Maggie stared at the gorgeous sunset in awe. When was the last time she'd watched the sunset? Knowing her schedule, probably never.

"That's our boat," he said as they hopped out of the car. He nodded to the sleek white speedboat docked at the end of the pier.

Maggie's throat bobbed as she gulped. "How familiar are you with current shipwreck statistics?"

"For the love of Pete, you've never been on a boat either?"

"No," she sighed.

He flashed a grin and took her hand, leading her down the sturdy wooden planks beneath their feet toward the boat. She seemed uneasy as she got in, but her expression brightened the moment the boat driver gave it some gas. The speedboat sliced through the calm water, which went from transparent turquoise to navy-blue under the darkening sky.

Ben slung an arm over Maggie's shoulders and enjoyed the

salty breeze hitting his face. The last time he'd been to the Bahamas was a year ago. He'd come here with Sonja Reyes, a Brazilian swimsuit model he'd briefly dated, and he'd been itching to come back ever since.

While the islands boasted plenty of celebrity-friendly resorts, Ben preferred Paradise Bay to all the others. It was subtle, certainly not as blatantly lavish as a place like Atlantis, but that's why Ben liked it. Private bungalows, deserted beaches, and best of all, the hotel was located near a wildlife preserve, making it hard for trespassers, aka paparazzi, to loiter around.

"Here we are, folks," the driver called over his shoulder as he slowed the boat and steered toward a long dock nearly hidden by thick foliage.

"Pass me your bag," Ben told Maggie.

She did, and he hopped onto the wooden pier and extended a hand to help her out. A tall blond man in a burgundy blazer materialized out of nowhere and strode toward them, greeting Ben with a firm handshake and dropping a polite kiss on Maggie's knuckles.

"I'm Marcus Holtridge, manager of Paradise Bay. Follow me."

He led them to a golf cart, sandwiched himself between them, and signaled the driver to go.

The golf cart maneuvered the lush grounds of the resort, and Ben felt a rush of satisfaction at the wonder dancing in Maggie's green eyes. He understood her reaction. The perfectly manicured lawns, the little cobblestone paths that wove through the luxurious setting, the bright exotic flowers that only added to the elegance of the spectacular layout. When Sonja first brought him here, he'd thought he'd died and gone to Eden.

They drove past a man-made waterfall that flowed into a small pond, and Maggie nudged his arm and gestured to the school of fat Koi swimming in the water. "Isn't that pretty?" she breathed.

He swept his gaze over her rosy cheeks and lit-up features. "Sure is."

As they entered the main section of the resort, Marcus pointed out various points of interest. The tennis courts, the spa, the small but elegant casino where Ben had lost five grand the last time he'd come.

It was the perfect place to relax without worrying about your face being splashed on every newspaper in the country and, considering he'd promised his agent he'd lay low, Ben couldn't have picked a better atmosphere to do it in.

Ten minutes later, the golf cart stopped in front of its destination. Maggie hopped out, followed by Marcus, while Ben fumbled with the overnight bag. He glanced over at the pale-yellow structure nestled between majestic fronds, feeling that same sense of amazement he'd experienced during his first visit. It wasn't the most magnificent bungalow, but it was picturesque and private and that's all Ben cared about. The little house stood on a stretch of clean white sand, steps away from the ocean, and if you left the windows open at night, the sound of waves lapping against the shore lulled you to sleep.

On the small porch of the bungalow, Ben accepted the key from Holtridge, thanked the man for his assistance, and then watched as the hotel manager and the golf cart disappeared down the path leading back to the main complex.

"This is beautiful," Maggie confessed as they stepped into the large spacious room.

A billowing white canopy hung from the ceiling and draped over the frame of the big mahogany bed, and on the blue bedspread sat a wicker basket filled with fragrant soaps, papaya shampoos, face towels and other welcome items.

Ben dropped the overnight bag on the polished hardwood floor. "You should see the hot tub."

"Hot tub?"

"Follow me."

He led her to the glass sliding door at the far end of the room and pointed.

"You've got to be kidding me," she said as her gaze followed his outstretched finger. Outside sat a four-person hot tub, skillfully built under a cluster of palm trees and surrounded by boulders, giving it the appearance of a natural rock pool.

"What do you say we get into our suits and hop in?"

"I didn't bring a suit."

Her disappointment pleased him. "Not to worry. When I asked the manager to leave a change of clothes in the closet, I made sure to request a few bikinis too. Go take your pick."

"How'd you pull all this together so quickly?"

He shrugged and offered a faint smile. "I'm Ben Barrett, remember?"

As Maggie drifted over to the tall oak armoire across from the bed, Ben walked toward the nightstand and reached for the telephone. "I'm going to make a quick call while you get changed."

He dialed his agent's number and waited. From the corner of his eye he saw Maggie grab one of the bathing suits off a hanger and—was she actually going into the bathroom to change? Yep.

Like he hadn't already seen her naked a dozen times.

A cheeky comment involving her initiation into the Mile High Club bit at his tongue, but Stu answered the phone before he could say it.

"Fuck, Ben, where are you now?"

"The Bahamas," he replied nonchalantly.

"Wonderful. Absolutely frickin' wonderful for you. It warms my heart that you're sun tanning on a beach while I'm working my ass off here."

"I thought you convinced the media I wasn't abducted."

"I did, but they still think you're up to something fishy. The prostitute angle is old news. So is elopement with the mysterious hotel chick. Now the consensus is that you're shacked up with another married broad."

"I was never shacked up with a married broad before."

"Of course not."

Ben's jaw tightened. Funny how Stu had been his agent for nine years and counting, yet the man still didn't have faith in him.

"There have been a few positive developments, though," Stu added, his tone all business now.

"Yeah, like what?"

"Two high-budget screenplays landed on my desk, and the studio contacted me about a sequel for *McLeod's Revenge*."

"Are you joking? *McLeod's Revenge Two*? The guy already got his damn revenge, what more is he after?"

"Who cares? It's money in our pockets."

Was it possible to loathe one little phrase this badly? He was so sick of talking about money. What happened to artistic expression? Thought-provoking, quality scripts? Challenging roles?

"Oh, and Alan Goodrich wants to meet with you."

Ben almost dropped the phone. "What?"

"He called to set up an appointment."

"Business or personal?"

"Seeing as you were screwing his wife, I doubt he wants to meet up so he can offer you a part in his new World War Two epic."

"Goodbye, Stu."

Ben hung up the phone before he said something he'd regret. His insides were tight with rage and churned with the slow boil of injustice he'd swallowed back for months now. If he wanted to, he'd phone up all the major tabloids and set them straight about Gretchen, the inheritance and the reasons behind the whole goddamn mess.

But he didn't want to.

Let the world think what they wanted of him. Let them say whatever they felt like saying about him. His private matters weren't anybody's business but his own.

"You okay?"

Maggie's soft voice brought him back to the present. She stood at the bathroom door, a towel wrapped around her waist and tucked under her breasts.

"I'm fine. Just checking in with my agent."

He stood up, tried to act like nothing was wrong, and probably succeeded. If there was one thing he was very good at, it was acting.

"Did I hear you talking about a movie sequel?" Her expression displayed curiosity. "That sounds cool."

He strode toward the armoire and rummaged around until he found a pair of swim trunks. Keeping to his word, Marcus Holtridge had also supplied him with a stack of clean clothing. Jeans, T-shirts, boxers, even a crisp black tuxedo draped on one of the hangers.

The tux gave him an idea, which he stored in the back of his brain as he quickly peeled off his shirt and unzipped his jeans.

"I guess it would be cool," he said in response to her remark, "if I wasn't turning down the part."

"Why would you turn down—" Her voice halted the second he dropped his pants.

Grinning at the tantalizing blush on her cheeks, Ben slowly slipped into his swim trunks, tugging at the material when it snagged over his growing erection.

"You have no shame," Maggie grumbled, openly staring at his cock.

"Nope." He tightened the drawstring and stepped toward her. "Now what do you say we get in the Jacuzzi and finish what we started on Papa G's jet?"

Maybe it made her the slut of the century, but Maggie had never been so excited to be naked before.

Well, not fully naked. She was wearing that indecent string bikini as she lowered her body into the hot bubbling water, and Ben had his trunks on as he quickly joined her, but they didn't need to be naked for her to know they were about to have wild, sweaty, hot tub sex. She honestly couldn't wait. Since she'd met Ben, she'd had sex in more new places than she could count— the shower, the kitchen counter, the living room floor, a private jet, for God's sake. Might as well add hot tub to the growing list.

"I want to tear that bikini off with my teeth."

"What?" Maggie shivered despite the near-boiling water lapping against her body.

Ben shot her an endearing smile. "Did I say that out loud?"

"Uh, yeah."

"Can't fault a guy for being honest."

"I guess not." She shifted so that one of the jets pressed directly against her tailbone, and her muscles turned to jelly as the pressure slowly massaged her skin. Overhead, a spatter of bright stars lit up the clear night sky. She tilted her head to take in the gorgeous view, breathing in the scent of salt and island freshness floating in the air.

This was nice. She hadn't wanted it to be nice, but it was. She hadn't taken a vacation in...well, she'd *never* taken a vacation, and the strange rush of relaxation coursing through her felt completely foreign.

"You're too far away," Ben complained.

With a roll of her eyes, she scooted over so they were side by side. Arm touching arm. Thigh against thigh.

He instantly draped one wet arm around her bare shoulders and slid his hand to give one of her breasts a firm squeeze. "Much better." He slanted his head and shot her a mischievous look. "Wanna make out?"

She laughed. "Sure. Maybe afterwards we could go to the malt shop and share a milkshake with two straws."

He didn't seem to mind her teasing. If anything, his grin only widened and, as usual, he wasted no time bending his head and covering her mouth with his.

She wasn't sure she'd ever get used to this man's kisses. So long and intoxicating. Hurried. Rough. Taking it slow? She doubted he knew what that meant. Oh no. His lips and tongue simply took what they wanted without permission.

Not that she minded. His hungry claim of her mouth stole the breath right out of her lungs and made her chest constrict with burning need. Each hot, toe-curling kiss ended with a gasp from her and a groan from him, and made her squirm under the warm water eddying around her.

149

Pulling back, Ben nipped playfully at her earlobe. "Why do you still have your suit on?"

"I'm waiting for you to tear it off with your teeth, remember?"

"Is that a challenge?"

"More like a dare."

"I like the way you think, Red."

Water splashed over the edge of the hot tub as Ben moved in front of her. He rested on his knees, his chiseled torso disappearing into the water with a splash of clear bubbles. "I'll begin with your bottoms," he said, his voice professional and matter-of-fact.

The last thing she saw before he ducked under the water was the tiny grin on his face. A second later, she jumped as his mouth latched onto her hip and tugged at the strings holding her bottoms together. His teeth grazed her skin. He tugged again and then one half of the triangle came loose.

Ben surfaced, wiping droplets off his somber face. "I'm sorry to inform you I couldn't save the knot to the right of your hip, Ms. Reilly. I do, however, have high hopes for the left one."

She choked back a laugh as he submerged again, and then shivered when he untied the second knot. Her bikini bottoms floated to the surface at the same time as Ben.

"Couldn't save the left one either. It's gone," he said, pointing to the shiny green material as a rush of water carried it away to the other side of the hot tub.

"You're a sad excuse for a doctor," she said with mock anger.

"That's what the producers at *General Hospital* said before they fired me," he answered with a rueful smile. "But it was only my second acting gig, so how could they blame me for being unable to pronounce Chronic Inflammatory Demyelinating Polyneuropathy?"

"What on earth is that?"

"To this day I still have no clue." He shrugged and then planted his gaze on her breasts, which were still covered. "I should take care of that."

He skimmed his fingers over her wet, fevered shoulders and swiftly maneuvered her so that her back was to him. She closed her eyes, inhaled deeply, waited for the sting of his teeth against her skin, and exhaled a shaky breath when her top came loose and her breasts were bared.

Her nipples instantly jutted out, hardening even more when she shifted and one of the jets sent a gushing rush of heat right against her breasts.

"So...your bathing suit has been removed," Ben whispered into her neck.

She twisted around to look at him. "Are you going to do that all night?"

"Do what?"

"Narrate."

"Why, does it turn you on?"

She paused. "I'm actually pretty indifferent to it."

"Indifferent?" His expression tightened with mock horror. "No woman of mine is ever allowed to feel indifference in my presence, sweetheart."

No woman of mine?

Before she could figure that one out, Ben dipped his head and brushed a light kiss over her lips. "Trust me, babe, by the time I'm finished with you, you're going to *love* my narration."

He cocked one dark brow and reassumed that professional demeanor. "I think it's time I paid some attention to—" he reached down and cupped her breasts, "—these."

A jolt of desire streaked across her chest, down her belly and settled into an impatient throb between her legs.

"Not sure what my opening move will be, though," he continued huskily. "Should I pinch?"

He rolled her nipples between his fingers and gave each pebbled nub a small pinch.

"Or squeeze?"

He squeezed.

"No, I've changed my mind. I think sucking will achieve the result I'm looking for."

With a roguish smile, he slid lower into the water and covered one breast with his mouth. A breath blew out of her mouth and dissolved into the steam rising from the hot tub. Ben's tongue began a torturous assault on her nipples, licking and swirling, laving and nipping.

And, each time, the pleasure became unbearable. Each time the scrape of his teeth brought a delicious sting of pain, he sucked it away. Sucked and kissed until she gave a primitive cry and sank under the water like a lump of clay.

With a chuckle, Ben grabbed her hips and brought her up. "I think it's time for my fingers to get involved," he said with a decisive nod.

The bubbles from the jets restricted her from seeing his hand, but she sure as hell felt it. Felt his fingers running down her throbbing slit, felt his thumb rubbing circles over her clit.

The throbbing grew worse. "No fingers," she choked out. "I need more."

"I'm sorry, we haven't reached that part of the narrative yet." He offered an apologetic shrug and continued his exploration of her pussy.

She groaned and fumbled for the waistband of his trunks. "I hate you."

"No you don't." He skillfully pushed her roaming hand away. "And stop interfering."

She almost bristled at his commanding tone but the hunger swarming his gaze stopped her. It was obvious he wanted her, and for a girl who'd never been wanted all her life, she received a sense of pride from his lust-filled expression.

She also received, after just a few short minutes of his finger sliding in and out of her, an orgasm. One that made her writhe and moan and shudder so hard she sent a tidal wave crashing over the side of the hot tub.

She gasped for air, inhaling a cloud of steam that warmed her cheeks. Heat consumed her body, heat from the fire burning inside her core, from the water splashing around her and the island breeze kissing her face.

"So, now I think that—" Ben started.

"Shut up. No more talking," she ordered, rising from the tub on unsteady feet.

"Where are you going?"

"Inside. Where I'm going to lie naked on the bed. And you're going to follow me, and take those damn trunks off, and then we're going to fuck each other's brains out." She rolled her eyes. "How's that for a narrative?"

Ben grinned. Without a word, he hopped out of the whirlpool, pinched her bare ass, and chased her into the bungalow. As she'd promised, she stretched out on the bed, naked and wet, watching as he reached for the waistband of his swimsuit. A second later, he was gloriously nude, all tanned skin and hard muscle, and so incredibly aroused her inner muscles gave an involuntary clench.

He stood there, silent and erect, and the teasing light left his blue eyes, replaced with a narrowed look of unrestrained sexual famine. She shivered under his hot stare, feeling like Little Red Riding Hood about to be consumed whole by the big bad wolf.

And oh, was Ben Barrett bad. Bad as he sheathed himself with a condom that seemed to materialize out of nowhere. Bad as he stepped toward the bed. So very *bad* as he lowered himself on top of her and rubbed the tip of his cock over her swollen pussy.

"Maggie," he rasped.

She waited for him to say something more, but he didn't. Instead, he tangled one hand in her damp hair, placed the other on her hip, and kissed her at the same time he drove deep inside her.

Her body stretched to accommodate him, and she instantly clamped her muscles over his shaft and arched her hips to bring him deeper. He groaned and dug his fingers into her waist, then slid all the way out only to pump right back in with a fast thrust.

Her eyes strayed to his biceps, where that tribal tattoo seemed to vibrate each time he flexed. Feeling unusually bold, she looped her arms around his neck, pulled him closer and ran her tongue over the black design inked on his arm.

His eyes narrowed into slits. "That's seriously hot, you know."

"That I'm licking your tattoo?" she murmured, continuing to trace the intricate pattern with the tip of her tongue.

"Uh-huh."

She moved her head and nibbled on his earlobe. "What about this? Is this hot?"

"Mmm-hmmm."

He stopped moving inside her, and she could feel his erection throbbing inside her unbelievably wet pussy.

"You're close, aren't you, Ben?" Oh man, did that throaty femme-fatale voice actually belong to *her*?

He responded with a mumbled expletive.

Smiling, she slid her hands down his sinewy back and grabbed his taut buttocks. "What are you waiting for then?"

"You."

"Me what?"

"I'm waiting for you to tell me just how much you want it." He rotated his hips and then withdrew again, his pace excruciatingly slow.

A shockwave rocked her core, causing her to squeeze his tight ass and buck against him. Suddenly she didn't have the energy to tease or lick or prolong the inevitable.

"I want it very, very badly," she choked out.

With a satisfied nod, he plunged into her again and swallowed her strangled cry with a hard kiss.

Sense of time and place eluded her as he pounded into her, as his mouth devoured hers and his fingers stroked her hair and her clit. She met his every thrust with the bucking of her hips, drank in his kisses, cried out his name. Waves of pleasure crashed over her. Perpetual. Unending. A climax so intense and extraordinary that her legs started to shake and shards of bright light exploded in front of her eyes.

The bliss only deepened when she felt Ben shudder, when she heard that low groan signaling his climax. She tightened her grip around his neck. When she pressed her breasts to his sweat-soaked chest, the erratic thumping of his heartbeat vibrated against her skin, making her own pulse race.

She didn't know how long they lay there, and she didn't care that the crush of his powerful chest restricted the flow of oxygen to her brain. She liked the weight of him. And the slick feel of him. And the spicy masculine scent of him. She knew she should move, get up, get dressed, put an end to this intimate moment, but she couldn't bring herself to do it. Instead, she released a sigh and stroked his back, pressing her face to his chest as he slowly rolled over and brought her with him.

Next to her, Ben moistened his dry lips, reeling not so much from his climax but from Maggie's odd behavior. Something had changed. He couldn't quite put his finger on it, but he sensed it as he held Maggie in his arms and threaded his fingers through her damp red hair. Somehow, in the ten minutes they'd lain there recovering from those mind-blowing orgasms, she'd dropped her guard. She hadn't jumped out of the bed after the sex, hadn't started rambling on about her schedule and schoolwork and all the reasons why being here with him was a bad idea.

She just lay there and let him stroke her hair.

He liked it.

A lot.

"So what now?" she asked after giving a big yawn. "Should we take a walk on the beach?"

"Says the redhead after yawning her face off," he teased. "It's okay to be tired, babe. To just lie around and do nothing."

She shifted, moving onto her side so that her gaze locked with his. Her expression reflected uneasiness. "Doing nothing makes me anxious."

He smiled. "I've noticed."

"It's not a bad thing, is it?"

"No, it's not a bad thing. No need to get defensive." He

reached for her leg and lifted it so that it draped over his, not sure why he needed the physical contact so desperately. "I just think you need to learn how to relax every now and then."

She didn't answer, but the troubled look on her face spoke volumes. He wondered how many times she'd heard that before from the people in her life. Her friends. Co-workers. Tony. Though he wasn't sure why, Ben suddenly grew certain that Maggie's non-existent love life was a direct result of her need to always be *doing* something.

"What do you want from your life?" he found himself blurting. "Aside from being a social worker?"

Surprise flickered in her gaze, followed by a glimmer of confusion. "To be honest, I've never really thought past the career thing."

"You don't think about getting married? Or having children? Or heck, traveling, gardening, anything that doesn't involve working?"

"Not really." Before he could question the response, she turned the tables on him. "What about you? Do you ever think of a life beyond acting?"

"All the time." A wry smile creased his mouth. "If I'm being honest, I'd tell you acting is definitely not what I'd thought it would be."

"What did you hope to get from it?"

He paused to think about the question. Shit. He'd never let himself examine the hopes he'd had going into it. Or the unhappiness he felt now that his career had zigzagged in a direction he'd never wanted.

"Ben?"

He bit the inside of his cheek, trying to put it into words he'd never said out loud. "It's...it's like I bought a first-class ticket for passage on the Titanic," he finally said. "You know, boarding the ship, getting caught up in the splendor of it, thinking I'm on top of the world. And then comes the iceberg and the ship sinks."

"So what's your iceberg?" she asked, reaching out to touch his chin.

He hadn't shaved in days, and the feel of Maggie's fingers skimming his rough beard made his groin tighten. She didn't miss the way his cock jerked in response, but she wiggled her eyebrows and shot him a no-nonsense stare. "Oh no. We're having a conversation. Stop trying to distract me."

He grinned. "I didn't do anything."

"No, but *he* did." She stared at his erection for a moment, and then shook her head as if to snap herself out of it. "So...the iceberg?"

"Being typecast," he admitted. "I started acting because I loved it, but I also wanted to be recognized. Respected. Then I did one action flick and suddenly I'm known as bad boy macho man Ben Barrett. I haven't been offered a decent role in years, Maggie. All I get are mindless let's-blow-up-every-possible-thing-we-can films."

She gave a dry smile. "Not that I have much experience in the movie industry, but one thing I've learned in life is that nobody's going to give it to you. If you want something, you go after it."

"I'm trying," he answered in frustration.

"Try harder."

Amazement washed over him. Damn, Maggie Reilly really was something. The women he knew would've done one of two things—laughed it off and told him to enjoy the money, or made a heartfelt speech about how one day someone would recognize his talent and give him a significant role. Not Maggie. Nope, she told him to try harder.

Oddly enough, it was just what he wanted—and needed—to hear.

She yawned again, the delicate muscles in her face stretching with fatigue. "You're right. I'm tired," she announced. "No beach walking tonight."

They were both still naked, but Maggie didn't seem to mind. Without an ounce of bashfulness, she stretched her arm out and fumbled on the end table for the remote control.

"I haven't watched TV in ages," she confessed with a tiny smile.

Although Ben would have liked to indulge in a repeat performance of what they'd done a half hour ago, he decided to let Maggie enjoy herself. If watching television would finally make her relax, he was willing to do it.

When she flicked on the TV, however, what flashed across the screen was not a mindless sitcom or movie of the week, but Ben's face.

"Hey, it's one of your movies," Maggie exclaimed. Before he could object, she raised the volume and the crack of gunfire filled the bungalow. "Huh. You're right about all the explosions."

Seeing his latest film play across the screen left Ben weary, but Maggie seemed to be enjoying it so he stayed quiet. He pulled her closer, wrapping one arm around her, and then turned his gaze to the movie, inwardly cringing at every loud blast and the sound of screeching tires from the car chase he'd loathed shooting.

The film dragged on, and next to him Maggie's naked body grew warmer and her breathing evened out. She'd fallen asleep. He tried to fight back that prickle of insult but it was hard. Hell, his movies sucked so bad they even made Maggie, the

159

workaholic Energizer bunny, fall asleep. That hurt more than he'd ever admit.

Trying not to jolt her, he slowly reached for the remote control next to her sleeping body and flicked off the TV. Then he reached for the lamp beside him and turned that off too. Darkness draped the room, save for one clear shaft of moonlight that poured in through the sheer curtains.

With a sigh, Ben closed his eyes and touched Maggie's hair again.

Just as he started to drift off, her soft voice broke through the silence in the room.

"You're a good actor, Ben," she murmured before making a breathy little noise and falling back into slumber.

Chapter Ten

"I don't think I'll ever get used to this," Maggie declared the next evening.

She collapsed on the bed, her stomach full from the eight-course dinner they'd just indulged in and her skin pink from the hours they'd spent in the sun earlier in the day.

"Get used to what?" Ben closed the door of the bungalow and headed for the plush leather armchair near the bed. He dropped into it with a contented sigh.

"This." She waved her hand around. "Our own private bungalow. Our own private stretch of sand. Being waited on at dinner. Eating steak and lobster."

Having wild, almost hourly sex with a movie star...

"And to think," Ben said with a chuckle, "we still have the whole night in front of us. You should hop in the shower, by the way. It's almost time."

Her head came up with a jerk. "Almost time for what?"

"It's a surprise."

"You know I don't like surprises."

"And I don't like tennis, but I played a few sets with you, didn't I?"

The memory brought a smile to her lips. Earlier she'd told Ben she hadn't played tennis since high school, and although he'd griped and grumbled the entire time, he'd spent two hours on the court with her, which was pretty sweet coming from a man who could barely serve the ball without hitting the net. Still, she'd found his pitiful tennis skills—and candid admission of inadequacy—seriously charming.

Stretching out her legs, she propped herself up on her elbows and sighed. "I'm too full to move. I'll shower later."

"No time. We're on a schedule, Red."

"Oh, are we?"

"Yep." He rose from his chair and gave one of her arms a tug, dragging her off the bed. "So get your pretty little ass into that shower."

"You're not going to join me?"

He shook his head. "There are a few details I need to take care of."

She couldn't help but pout. "Fine."

Getting to her feet, she drifted into the bathroom. She slipped out of her yellow sundress and hung it on the hook behind the door, then stepped into the black-tiled shower stall next to the marble bathtub. As the warm water sluiced over her sun-kissed body, she lathered lavender body wash on her skin, which was still slick and smooth from the pounds of tanning lotion she'd rubbed on it.

She hadn't felt this relaxed in years. Actually, she hadn't felt this relaxed *ever*, seeing as her life was a big ball of stress that revolved around work and school. Relaxation had never been part of the equation.

Don't forget that.

Her hand trembled as she flipped open the lid of the shampoo bottle and squirted a glop in her palm. That cynical little voice in her head was right. Enjoying her time at the resort, her time with Ben, was one thing, but she couldn't forget where she came from. What she'd be going back to when this trip ended.

Her schedule, not to mention her finances, didn't allow for impromptu island getaways and sweaty sex with celebrities. It was easy to lose herself in these luxurious surroundings, but luxury wasn't something she could count on.

What happened if she lost her job or failed her exams? Ben had his big pile of money to cushion his fall, but what did she have?

Herself. No family, no roots, no security blankets. She had only herself, and she needed to remember that before she got caught up in all this glitz and glamour.

Before she started to believe that a girl like her might actually belong in Ben Barrett's life.

"Mimi is here to do your hair and makeup."

Maggie moved her gaze from her newly polished fingernails and fought back a yawn. "Is he trying to kill me?"

Denise, the petite blonde who'd been shuffling Maggie around the spa for the past couple of hours, gave a rueful smile. "Wow, you really are one of those women who can't handle being pampered," she remarked with a teasing lilt to her voice.

"So that's what you call being poked and prodded for two hours? Pampered?"

Denise wagged her finger. "Don't pretend you didn't like it. I saw your face during that mud bath. You enjoyed it." She took a step back. "I'll send Mimi in."

Maggie waited for Denise to leave the spa's sitting room before releasing a sigh of contentment. Fine, so she'd enjoyed the mud bath. And the massage from Paulo the Latin heartthrob. Maybe even the manicure and pedicure.

Okay, she'd enjoyed it all.

When Ben had dropped her off at the spa, she'd ordered herself to have a bad time. To hate every second of the spa experience and laugh in the face of luxury. But she'd failed. She felt like Cinder-freaking-ella, and God help her, but she'd wholeheartedly relished every tranquil, self-indulgent moment.

"I'm here to do your hair." A willowy brunette with a stunning olive complexion strode into the room carrying a large silver case in one hand.

"Why exactly am I getting my hair done again?"

Mimi shrugged. "Afraid I don't know. Mr. Barrett never said."

"Of course he didn't."

Maggie settled back in the plush leather chair and decided there was no point questioning Ben's motives. She didn't voice one complaint, not even when Mimi nearly scalped her trying to twist her unruly hair into a French twist. Didn't flinch either, when the woman went at her eyebrows with a pair of mean-looking tweezers.

An hour later, Mimi finished styling her hair and applying her makeup, but just when Maggie got to her feet thinking they were done, the woman held up her hand.

"One more thing."

She pinched the bridge of her nose, the one part of her face she could touch without ruining her makeup. "I've been in this spa for *three* hours, what more can he want to do to me?"

Mimi smiled, left the room, and quickly returned with a garment bag and a shoebox. "He wants you to get dressed."

She would've made another sarcastic comment if it weren't

for the spectacular item of clothing the hairstylist removed from the bag. Maggie took a breath, eyes wide as she stared at the slinky, emerald-green dress. It was gorgeous, more gorgeous than anything she owned. Or had ever owned.

"Versace's fall line," Mimi supplied, seeing the wonder in her eyes. "Hasn't even hit the racks yet." She draped the dress over the back of the chair. "I'll leave you to get dressed."

The second the door closed, Maggie wasted no time pulling off her jeans. Getting her tank top off without ruining her new updo and impeccable makeup proved to be a challenge, but she managed. She carefully wiggled into the Versace masterpiece, and then spun around to examine her reflection in the full-length mirror across the sitting room.

Wow.

No, make that a double wow.

With her hair piled atop her head, with all that sooty mascara coating her lashes, and with the gorgeous satin material clinging to her curves, she looked like a different person.

"Oh my, I believe Mimi deserves a raise."

Denise's voice came from the doorway, and Maggie blushed as she met the blonde's admiring stare. "You think I look good?"

"I think you look fabulous," Denise corrected. She gave one last appraising look, and then gestured for Maggie to follow her. "Mr. Barrett asked for you to meet him in the lobby at midnight. You don't want to be late."

Maggie glanced down at her bare feet. "But I don't have shoes."

Denise pointed to the shoebox the hairdresser had left behind. "Sure you do."

Feeling like a kid on Christmas morning, Maggie made a

beeline for the narrow box. She opened it, and unlike the hand-me-down gifts she'd received from her foster families over the years, this box contained something new and shiny. Silver, high-heeled sandals that matched the silver eye shadow Mimi had dabbed on Maggie's eyelids. Ben had obviously planned everything to a T.

She slipped on the shoes and followed Denise out the door, oddly self-conscious as they left the spa. Her heels clicked against the white marble floor beneath them, and her heartbeat drummed in her throat as they neared the majestic lobby of the Paradise Bay resort.

"I feel like a princess," she whispered, shooting a nervous glance at the woman next to her.

Denise stopped in front of the marble arch leading into the lobby. "And there's your prince," she whispered back.

Maggie shifted her gaze and saw him. Leaning casually against one of the stone pillars in the middle of the large room, his hawk-like gaze drilling into her.

Her surroundings seemed to fade as their eyes locked, and she never broke the contact as she walked across the room toward Ben.

"You look...damn, Maggie," he murmured as she approached. "You look beautiful."

Heat spilled through her at Ben's speechless reaction. She had to admit, as out of her depth as she felt in the elegant dress he'd bought for her, she liked the effect it had. The neckline dipped so low that her breasts practically spilled out of the silk bodice, and that slit up the side showed a hell of a lot of thigh. It was the kind of dress meant to tease a man into submission, and though she'd never be a hundred percent comfortable dressing like a vixen, she liked the delight she saw in Ben's dark blue eyes.

She also liked the tuxedo currently hugging his lean body, the way the black jacket stretched over his broad shoulders and emphasized his rock hard chest. With that classy tux and his clean-shaven face, he looked every inch the movie star he was, and again she felt like Cinderella as she accepted his proffered arm and curled her fingers around his biceps.

"Did you have fun at the spa?" he asked as they fell into step together.

"Yes."

"Good."

He led her across the lobby toward a set of heavy oak doors flanked by two large men in tuxedos. At their approach, the men pulled the doors open with a graceful swoop and gestured for them to enter. Seeing as they were dressed like they were going to the prom, Maggie expected to walk into a grand ballroom. To her surprise, it was a casino.

And not the kind of casino you saw in Las Vegas tourism commercials, with flashing neon lights and ear-piercing sounds jangling out of slot machines. Small and sophisticated, this one offered a fair amount of game tables, waiters with trays of champagne, and a black tie clientele. Aside from the occasional jubilant cry coming from the roulette section, the atmosphere was serious yet relaxed, and it practically oozed money.

"Do you like to gamble?" Ben asked as they crossed the plush carpeted floor toward one of the blackjack tables.

"I don't know. I've never gambled before."

What would I have to gamble with? she almost added, but stopped herself just in time. A man as wealthy as Ben wouldn't understand, anyway.

"Trust me. You'll like it."

They paused in front of a table, and a man in a black suit

approached and exchanged a few words with Ben. They spoke in murmured tones, but Maggie caught the word "markers" and then raised her brows at the number "two thousand".

As the bow-tied card dealer doled out a stack of chips and placed them in front of Ben, she leaned over and whispered, "Did you just ask for two thousand dollars worth of chips?"

"Yep." He split the stack in half and pushed one pile toward her. "This one's yours."

She gulped. "I can't take your money. What if I lose?"

"Then you lose."

Her throat tightened with irritation. "I won't be in debt to you, Ben."

"Call it a gift."

"A thousand-dollar stack of chips is not a gift." Setting her jaw, she pushed the red circles back toward Ben's pile. "I can't accept it."

He paused for a moment, and then sighed. "Fine, be difficult. We'll play as a team."

"And I don't keep a dime of the winnings," she added, her tone firm.

"And you won't keep a dime of the winnings," he echoed grudgingly.

The card dealer's lips twitched, and Maggie suspected he found the entire exchange amusing. He'd probably never encountered a woman so willing to kiss a thousand bucks goodbye.

"Ready to play some cards?" the man asked, glancing from her to Ben.

They spent the next hour at the blackjack table, with Ben explaining the game to her with the utmost of patience. After a few big wins, Maggie started to relax. She smiled at the tuxedo-clad men who joined them, sipped a glass of champagne, and stared at a familiar-looking woman in a gold sequined dress for ten minutes before Ben finally whispered that she was the lead anchor for NBC's evening news.

"You do watch the news, don't you?" he teased.

"Sometimes."

The laugh he gave sent a flurry of shivers up her spine. "Don't you feel alienated sometimes, being so out of touch with the world?"

She shrugged. "I'm too busy to feel alienated."

He tweaked one of the wavy tendrils framing her cheeks. "We really need to talk about this jam-packed schedule of yours."

Maggie's reply was cut off by the sound of a throaty female voice squealing, "Benjamin?"

An unbelievably tall, unbelievably beautiful woman with raven hair and sparkling blue eyes sauntered over in an indecent red dress and a pair of three-inch heels. Before Maggie could blink, the giant sexpot threw her arms around Ben and splattered kisses on his cheeks.

"Benjamin! It is you!" With her heavy South American accent, it sounded more like "Ben-ja-meeen, eet eeez you!" Something about the way the woman's eyes twinkled suggestively hinted that this beauty knew Ben on a very intimate level. In fact, at a closer examination of the black-haired beauty's face, Maggie realized she was the supermodel at Ben's side in the picture she'd found on the Internet.

"Sonja," Ben said in a warm voice, gingerly disentangling himself from the woman's embrace, "I should've known I'd run into you here."

"Well, of course. This is my second home. Do you

remember when we summered here, Benjamin?" Sonja licked her bottom lip, a move so blatantly sexual Maggie wanted to tear out the woman's tongue.

Meow.

"And who is your lovely friend?" Sonja added.

Maggie had to hand it to the woman. She made the phrase "lovely friend" seem like the most contemptible insult ever composed.

"This is Maggie Reilly." Ben's features looked strained, his discomfort evident in his eyes.

"It is wonderful to meet you, Maggie."

Damn, even her name coming out of Sonja's lush red lips sounded like an affront.

"Yeah, same here," she replied.

"And are you also a model, Maggie?"

She swallowed, feeling horribly exposed as Sonja looked her up and down. "Actually, I'm a waitress. From New York."

There was a moment's silence, finally broken by a long tinkling laugh from Sonja, who turned to grin at Ben. "So you're—how do you Americans say it? Slumming it?"

The callous words sliced into Maggie's chest like a blade and caused her breath to jam in her throat. She no longer felt exposed. She felt gutted, humiliated, and even though nobody was looking their way, she felt like every eye in the room was glued on her.

Her hands started to tremble. She wanted to reply with a catty comment, slap this Brazilian bitch the way she'd slapped Robbie Hanson when he'd called her a foster-freak back in the ninth grade, but for the life of her she couldn't make her vocal cords work.

So she did the only other thing she could think of. She

straightened her back, lifted her chin and walked away as steadily as her legs would allow and with as much dignity as she could muster.

"Oopsy. I seem to have upset your little friend."

Ben's heart shrank in his chest as he stared after Maggie's retreating back. Next to him, Sonja looked pleased as punch, which made him rethink every positive thing he'd ever thought of the woman. She was a snob, yes. Self-absorbed, totally. But he'd never taken her for downright cruel.

"That was uncalled for," he snapped.

Sonja just laughed. "Oh, Benjamin, I was only—how do you say?—goofing around. Your friend is much too sensitive. This is why you need a real woman, *caro.*"

The air sizzled from the hot sparks of fury he shot in his former flame's direction. "I have a real woman." He hooked his thumb at the exit. "She went thataway."

Without another word, he left Sonja by the blackjack table and marched out of the casino, quickening his stride when he entered the lobby and found it empty. One of the clerks at the front desk discreetly nodded toward the glass doors at the lobby's entrance.

Ben stepped outside just in time to see Maggie stalking towards the golf cart parked in front of the building. She looked so achingly beautiful in that green dress, so goddamn sexy in those strappy heels, that he had to restrain himself from pulling her into his arms. She wasn't crying, but the look of ice she gave him when she noticed his presence clearly said *back off.*

"Maggie..." he began timidly.

She bunched the hem of her dress with her hands so it wouldn't drag on the cement on her way to the waiting cart.

"Don't bother. It's not your fault she spoke the truth."

He almost keeled over backwards. "What? You think what she said was the tru—"

He quit talking when he saw her flop onto the back of the golf cart and signal the driver. Chest tight with anger, he pushed forward and leaped into the cart before it sped off.

He shifted so that he faced Maggie and forced himself to take a calming breath, but it didn't ease the tension constricting his jaw.

"There wasn't an ounce of truth to what Sonja said," he snapped, stunned that Maggie would even suggest such a thing.

"Maybe not. But it is something I've been wondering myself. What are you doing with me, Ben? You're a big movie star, I'm a waitress. You've got ten million dollars in your bank account, I'm lucky to see a hundred in mine. You know Brazilian supermodels and bling rappers, I spend my days with poor and abused kids."

She let out a strangled sigh and scrunched up the material of her dress with one hand. "This isn't me, Ben. This dress. Being pampered in a spa. Throwing away money at casinos. It's not *me*, and you don't seem to get that."

"I don't seem to get it?" he echoed, growing angry. "Why would I? From the day we met I've been trying to impress you! Since nothing else seemed to work, I thought whisking you away to a tropical resort might."

"Why would you want to impress me?" Her voice came out strained. "I...I don't get what you want from me, Ben."

He could see her pulse thudding in her throat, could hear the ragged breaths exiting her mouth, and a thread of confusion stitched his insides. She'd just raised the one question he'd been avoiding for days.

What did he want from her?

Sex would've been the answer a week ago.

More sex would've been the answer last night.

Yet, if he were honest with himself, he'd admit that it had always been about more than sex. He'd liked Maggie from the moment he met her. Liked her sass, her confidence, her complete disinterest in his celebrity. He liked that she wasn't scared to tell him off, and he especially liked how she made him *work*. For her body, her trust, her time.

Women constantly threw themselves at his feet, but not Maggie. She knew who she was and what she wanted, and she wasn't afraid to say it. That's probably what he liked most of all.

"I want to be with you." He raked his fingers through his hair, frazzled. "I'm with you because I like you. Because you're...*real*. Don't you get it? I'm surrounded by plastic people. Fake, shallow people who think they know me, who pretend they *care* about knowing me. Do you realize you're the first person other than a reporter who actually wanted to know where I grew up?"

She didn't answer.

"Hell, even my own agent doesn't bother to dig deeper." His mouth twisted in a bitter frown. "He hasn't once asked for details about my recent inheritance. He just assumes—like the rest of the world—that I fucked Gretchen Goodrich."

"And you expected something different?" Her voice sounded cool. "You've got a reputation for sleeping around, it's not so shocking that people believe you went to bed with a married woman."

Something inside him hardened. "And what about you, Maggie? Do you believe that line of bull?"

"I don't know what to believe. I don't know you, Ben,

outside of the biblical sense, anyway."

His nostrils flared at her dismissive tone. "And in the entire week we've spent together, you didn't get a sense of who I am, that I might be a decent guy?"

She tilted her head and shot him a look full of distress and far too much wisdom for her age. "Very few people are decent, Ben. In the end, the only person you can count on is yourself. Sex, relationships, even love, they're not tangible, they disappear in the blink of an eye."

"So what, you avoid it all for fear that it might disappear?" He shook his head. "Is that why you hide behind your job and your volunteer work and school, because those are the only things you can count on?"

She just frowned.

"Well, I say it's bullshit," he continued, gulping in the late night air. "You *can* count on relationships and other people to be there for you. Some connections can never be broken. Take my mother, for instance. She had a hard life, raised me on her own, struggled to put food on the table, and she never complained, never packed up and left, even though I know there were times she must have felt like it."

"You want to talk about mothers, Ben?" Maggie shot back, pure venom lining her voice. "Well, mine abandoned me in front of a convenience store when I was five. She told me to wait outside while she went over to the bank, said she'd be back in ten minutes. You know how long I waited out there for her?"

He faltered, completely taken aback by the shards of raw pain slicing her features.

"Thirteen hours. I waited for thirteen hours before the owner of the store finally called the cops, who carted me off to social services."

The driver pulled the little cart to a stop in front of their bungalow, and Maggie hopped out without another word. Quietly thanking the man behind the wheel, Ben shoved his hands in the pockets of his trousers and climbed the porch with slow, heavy steps. Maggie was already inside by the time he entered the room, but he still had no idea what to say to her.

Her confession reverberated through his head. It brought a knot of sickness to his stomach, a tight squeeze to his heart, and for a moment he had to wonder how this perfect night he'd planned had ended up in shambles.

Ben couldn't wrap his brain around it. His own father had walked out on him, but growing up with a warm, loving mother had dulled the ache his dad's desertion had left in his heart. He couldn't even imagine how Maggie must feel, knowing she'd been abandoned on the sidewalk like a piece of trash.

"I lived in sixteen foster homes during the thirteen years I was part of the system," she said, continuing as if they'd never been interrupted.

She paused in front of the armoire and reached for the overnight bag she'd stowed on the bottom shelf. As she rummaged in the bag, she glanced at him over her shoulder, her expression unreadable. "I've been on my own since I was five years old, Ben, so don't talk to me about connections and lasting relationships. In my life, there's no such thing."

Chapter Eleven

The Gulfstream jet cruised the morning sky at thirty-thousand feet, heading back in the direction of New York, but Maggie couldn't decide if she was looking forward to the prospect of going home, or dreading it. The events of last night still haunted her. Sonja's harsh words, the blow-up with Ben that followed. He hadn't tried to kiss or touch her after that, just slid into bed and went to sleep, while Maggie lay awake half the night and thought about everything she'd said to him.

Her head told her she'd spoken the truth, and years of being alone only strengthened her belief that relying on others was a mistake. Yet her heart spoke differently. Her heart argued that she shouldn't allow the past to affect her future. That sooner or later she'd need to lower the walls she'd raised and let someone in.

It was funny, really. She'd tried to explain to Ben why she was keeping him at arm's length, and in the process she'd ended up doubting her own convictions. She'd always told herself she needed to secure her career before thinking about relationships, about marriage and babies, but now she wasn't so sure.

Was she simply using her goals as an excuse not to get close to someone? What about when she earned her degree and started her social work? Would she finally open her heart and seek out love, or would she merely find another goal to fixate on as a means of avoidance?

All troubling questions, ones she'd never asked herself before, and she found it ironic that an arrogant movie star had been the one to spur this internal investigation. Celebrities were supposed to be superficial, preoccupied with material things and trivial matters, and though it shamed her to admit it, that was partly what attracted her to Ben in the first place. She'd figured he'd tire of her after a day or two, and then be on his way. That he hadn't was probably the most troubling thing of all.

Leaning back in her chair, Maggie raised her hands and rubbed her temples, excruciatingly aware of Ben's presence.

Sitting there in a black long-sleeve shirt and black jeans, with morning stubble dotting his chin and dark hair falling onto his forehead, he looked sexy and dangerous, reminding her of how attracted she was to him. But he hadn't said a word since they'd boarded the jet, and the silence between them had dragged on for so long she had no clue how to make it go away.

She didn't know what to say to him, didn't know how she felt about him, and she'd never dealt well with uncertainties.

"Gretchen was the other woman."

Her head jerked up. "What?" She met his gaze, not sure if he'd spoken or if she'd imagined it.

"Remember I said my father ran off with another woman? Well, it was Gretchen Goodrich."

She had no idea how to respond to that so, as usual, she took the easy route. "Oh."

Ben shifted in his seat, crossed one leg over the other and inhaled deeply. He looked as troubled as she felt, and she resisted the urge to lean over and kiss his troubles away. That would probably be inappropriate, anyway, considering the bomb he'd just dropped.

"My father was always looking for a get-rich scheme, according to my mom. After he got Mom pregnant, he searched for any reason to get away from her. Spending the rest of his life in Cobb Valley, stuck with a wife and a kid, didn't appeal to him. So he made excuses to leave, phony business trips, visits to non-existent relatives. Apparently he met Gretchen during a trip to Vegas. She was nineteen at the time, vacationing with her family."

Maggie paused. "The Hunters, right? I read on the 'Net that they own a salad dressing empire or something."

"You read right." Ben's mouth twisted in a wry smile. "I'm sure that's what attracted my father to her in the first place."

"So they got together?"

"They got *married*," he corrected. "Of course, dear Dad neglected to tell his new wife that he'd already tied the knot with someone else."

"What happened?" she asked, curious.

"Long story short, Gretchen and my father were married for two years before her parents finally stepped in. They weren't pleased with the marriage to begin with, but once my father tried to control the trust fund Gretchen received when she turned twenty-one, her father did some digging and found out about my mother and me. They had him arrested."

"For...bigamy?"

"Theft, actually. When the truth came out that his marriage to Gretchen wasn't legal, he tried to run off with a wad of cash and some of her jewelry. He was behind bars for a few years." Ben let out a sigh. "He had a heart attack in prison and died."

"Did you and your mother know about Gretchen?"

"Mom did, but she never told me, and the Hunters made

sure to keep the scandal under wraps. I only found out when Gretchen contacted me six months ago. She was diagnosed with breast cancer, and she'd been thinking about her life, her past. She said she'd never stopped feeling guilty for being the reason my dad abandoned his family. I guess that's why she wrote me into her will."

Ben reached for the coffee cup on the poker table and took a long sip. He set down the cup and glanced over with a pained expression. He looked so solemn, so downcast, that this time she didn't stop herself from reaching over and touching him. She squeezed his hand and then interlaced their fingers.

"So why didn't you just tell the truth, to the press, I mean?"

His fingers tightened over hers. "I thought about it, but there was my mom to consider."

"What do you mean?"

"Gretchen left me that fortune to ease her own guilt, but to me, it's just a reminder of what a cad of a father I had. Money isn't going to make the memories go away, especially for my mother." Ben let out a strangled groan. "Damn it, just knowing the money will be released to me after Gretchen's estate goes through probate makes me feel like I'm betraying my mom. Like I'm profiting from her pain."

Oh God. The vulnerability etched on his features left Maggie speechless. How was this the same man who'd practically ordered her to give him a place to stay? How was this the same man whose arrogance drove her crazy?

"Not to mention," he added, "if I tell the media the truth about Gretchen and me, the vultures will camp out on my mom's doorstep and demand to know how she feels knowing her husband left her for an heiress. I can't do that to her." He released a heavy sigh. "Let the press think what they want of me, as long as they leave my mother alone."

Maggie swallowed. Hard. Once, twice. After the third gulp she stopped fighting herself and leaned forward to plant a soft kiss on his lips.

"What was that for?" Ben murmured after she'd pulled back.

She sighed. "That was for being far more decent than I gave you credit for, Ben."

The second they stepped out of the gate at the airport, Ben saw the reporters. Rather than the usual folks waiting for friends and families to walk out of the gate, they were greeted by a crowd of vultures with microphones and cameras. Angry flashbulbs exploded in front of his eyes. A slew of questions assaulted his ears, each one bringing a jolt of fury.

He swallowed back the rage and glanced over at Maggie, who looked startled. Her green eyes widened as the mob closed in on them. "What the..."

"Move," he ordered before she could finish the shocked sentence.

He held onto her arm and practically dragged her toward the exit. The press stayed on their heels, capturing their every move with those intrusive cameras. They were in a large open space but Ben suddenly felt like the entire airport was closing in on him and he quickened his strides, loosening his grip on Maggie's arm when he noticed his knuckles had turned white and were digging into her skin.

"Enjoy your vacation, Ben?" one obnoxious reporter called out.

Another followed up with, "Maggie, how long have you two been seeing each other?"

How the fuck did they know Maggie's name? Without pausing to question the woman who'd spoken, Ben pushed Maggie through the automatic doors. Her eyes were still wide with distress, but she didn't say a word. Just glanced back at the reporters still trailing after them, her face flickering with disbelief and confusion. She looked dazed, stunned, and he didn't blame her. He'd gotten used to this bullshit years ago, but he understood how it could be overwhelming for someone else.

He took her hand and pulled her toward a taxi, waited for her to get in then slid inside and slammed the door. Another flash caught his eye and he almost gave the finger to the reporter who'd snapped their picture.

Leaning back in his seat, he opened his mouth to address the driver, only to be cut off by Maggie. He was taken aback when she softly gave out directions to the Olive Martini.

As the cab pulled away from the airport, he looked at her and said, "Are you sure you want to go to work?"

"I don't have a choice," she said in a shaky voice. "My shift starts in an hour."

A short silence stretched between them. Maggie kept her gaze glued to the window, but he could tell she was still shaken up and confused by what just happened. He was pretty fucking confused himself. How had the press learned Maggie's identity? He hadn't told a soul that he was staying at her apartment, not even Stu or his publicist knew about her. And the resort would never have released the information—Marcus Holtridge and his staff respected their guests' privacy far too much to sell them out to the media, especially since the resort prided itself on secrecy.

Unless it wasn't a staff member who'd said anything, but another guest...

He stifled a groan as it hit him. Sonja. It had to be Sonja. She'd looked undeniably pissed when he'd left her in the casino after she'd offended Maggie, and he wouldn't put it past his ex-flame to get even by talking to a couple of reporters. He'd always told Sonja how much he hated the vultures, and if she wanted revenge for his rebuffing her, calling the press would be right up her alley.

The silence in the cab dragged on so long Ben began to feel claustrophobic again. He wanted to say something, but he feared anything he said would only push Maggie farther away from him. She'd been so happy and relaxed when he'd first brought her to the resort, and he knew she'd been having a good time, at least up until when they'd run into Sonja. But despite her shutting down afterwards, she'd seemed to come around again on the plane, when he'd told her the truth about Gretchen. He suspected they'd reached some kind of turning point, though he couldn't quite put a label on it yet. And now it was all blown to hell, thanks to a few nosy reporters.

He wanted to tell her he'd fix this, that somehow he'd make the media storm go away, but he knew better than to make empty promises. The press would hound him no matter what he did, and even if Stu and his publicist managed to spin the story in a way that made his relationship with Maggie not seem so tawdry, the reporters already knew her name. And that meant they'd soon learn everything else about her. Where she worked, where she lived.

And if he knew the vultures—and boy, did he know them—they wouldn't hesitate to make Maggie's life as hellish as they'd made his.

"You're late."

Maggie's head snapped up, her hand poised over the laces of her sneakers. In the doorway of the employee lounge, Linda stood with her arms crossed over her chest. She could tell from the look on her manager's face that she wasn't happy with her.

"I know, I'm sorry," she burst out, quickly kicking off her shoes and grabbing for the heels at the bottom of her locker. "It won't happen again."

"It'd better not." With a deep frown, Linda stalked off.

Ouch.

Maggie glanced at her watch, which confirmed what she already knew, that her shift had only started five minutes ago. Since when did Linda get so crabby over five measly minutes?

She would've arrived at the Olive sooner, but she and Ben had gotten stuck in traffic on the way back from the airport. And boy, had that been one awkward cab ride.

They hadn't said one word to each other, and she knew it was more her fault than his. After being barraged by those reporters at the airport—reporters who knew *her name*—she hadn't known what to say or how to react. The cameras, the photographers, the questions...it was all too overwhelming. Terrifying, if she were being honest. So she'd stayed silent, despite the fact that Ben looked desperate to talk about what happened.

Well, she wasn't ready to talk about it. Not now. Not when she had an entire evening of waitressing to get through, not when she still couldn't put into words how the sight of those reporters had made her feel.

Smothering a sigh, she finished dressing and tied her hair up into a ponytail. God, she didn't want to be here right now. How could she possibly focus on work when her body still felt bruised from all those reporters' questions, when her mind was still swimming with confusion about her feelings for Ben

Barrett?

The last thing she felt like doing was working, and the feeling only grew stronger when she stepped out of the lounge and realized the owner of the bar had finally decided to make an appearance. She gave a startled gasp as she bumped into Jeremy Henderson in the hallway.

"Hello, Mr. Henderson," she said quickly, struggling to tie her apron and keep a polite smile on her face at the same time.

He appraised her with a cool look. "You're late, Ms. Reilly."

"I know. It won't happen again," she said for the second time.

Without replying, he moved past her and rounded the counter, where he exchanged a few words with Matt.

She stifled another sigh. Great start to a shift, pissing off both her manager and the bar owner in less than the five minutes she was late by. Pausing at the counter, she grabbed an order pad and a tray, and turned around just in time to bump into Trisha.

Trisha?

"What are you doing here?" Maggie demanded. "Aren't you supposed to be at the puppet show? That's why you took my shift yesterday, right?"

Splotches of crimson stained Trisha's olive-colored cheeks. "Uh, I traded shifts with Kate. Lou cancelled tonight but we're going out to dinner tomorrow so I needed Kate to cover for me."

"Lou cancelled?"

"Um, yeah."

Disbelief and suspicion battled for her brain's attention. This whole shift switcheroo hadn't sat right with her from the beginning. "There was no musical, was there?" she said slowly.

Trisha's cheeks grew redder. "No," she finally admitted.

"But Lou and I really are going out tomorrow and it's the first time he's wanted to take me out to dinner in *ages* so I had to switch with Kate and—"

"I need to speak to both of you," their manager's voice interrupted Trisha before she could finish.

Linda stalked over, gesturing for them to follow her to the other end of the counter. With the Olive's owner out of earshot, Linda fixed both waitresses with a deadly stare. "I spend two hours every week writing up a damn schedule, and I won't have any of my employees screwing around with it at their leisure."

Trisha's flush deepened. "Linda—"

"Let me finish." The manager turned to Maggie. "The next time you decide to take a personal day, you clear it with me first, understand? You don't call Trisha and Kate and make changes to the schedule without speaking to me, Maggie."

She swallowed. "I..."

"And you," Linda cut in, turning to Trisha. "You don't take anyone's shift without asking me. Now both of you, get to work. Jeremy is here, so you had better be on your best behavior."

"What the hell is going on?" Maggie demanded after Linda marched away. "You never cleared it with Linda?"

"You can thank me later," Trisha shot back. "I just got bitched at by our boss so you could go on a romantic getaway with Tony."

Tony?

Trisha hurried off before Maggie could respond. Since she was fairly certain her manager's eyes were glued to her, Maggie gripped her order pad and headed toward one of her booths. She had to erase her customer's order three times before she got it right, but she couldn't force her bewildered mind to focus on work at the moment.

Trisha thought she'd gone away with Tony? Why would she think that? And how had she even known Maggie was away?

She drifted back to the counter and placed her drink orders with Matt, then curled her hands into fists as it dawned on her.

Ben.

Ben must have somehow contacted Trisha and asked her to cover last night's shift.

The sneaky bastard!

A slow rush of anger filled her veins and made her fingers tighten over the edge of her tray. Damn him. All she'd asked when she'd agreed to give him a place to stay was that he didn't complicate her life, and what had he done? He'd complicated her freaking life. Distracted her from her school work, stuck his nose into her job, and now her face would most likely be on every tabloid on the newsrack because of him. The attention at the airport had made her feel angry, exposed, and although she knew it wasn't Ben's fault the media had been waiting for them in the gate, she still blamed him just a little. She should've never gotten involved with a movie star. What the hell had she been thinking?

Her hands started to shake as she realized by now the entire world probably knew about her and Ben. What if the reporters started harassing her the way they harassed Ben? What if they showed up here at work, or at her apartment, or the community center? What if they dug around in her background, decided to paint her as some abandoned foster kid, or a gold-digger, or something equally horrendous?

The final thought made her hands tremble even more, which caused the tray she was holding to tilt over. The glasses on it slid around, screwing up the balance of the tray, and before she could stop it, three tall glasses of beer smashed onto floor. The glass shattered, cold liquid splashing against her ankles. She nearly gasped with embarrassment when she noticed the entire bar had gone dead silent. Customers were peering over to examine what had caused the commotion and all eyes were on her. She turned her head away from the curious stares and a second later she was on her knees, fumbling with the shards of glass with her bare hands.

A strong arm pushed her out of the way. "Careful, you'll cut yourself," Matt said anxiously. He'd brought a rag with him and began soaking up the spilled liquid.

"I'll clean it," she said, mortified by her clumsiness.

He pushed her hands away again. "Go clean yourself up," he returned. "There's beer dripping down your legs, Mags."

"Let me help—"

"I can handle it."

He looked ticked off with her and she didn't blame him. She'd made a huge mess and she felt terrible that Matt was the one cleaning it up.

She swallowed, then nodded, then rose to her feet. She saw Trisha by the counter, watching her with concern as she walked toward the employee lounge, but her friend didn't follow her, most likely because Trish didn't want to make any more waves with Linda. There was a small bathroom in the back of the lounge, and Maggie headed for it, pulling paper towels out of the dispenser and wiping down her beer-soaked ankles. When she exited the washroom, she found Jeremy Henderson waiting for her in the doorway.

"What the *hell* was that?" he demanded.

His harsh voice sent a cold knot of dread to her gut. The tall, balding man was absolutely seething as he entered. He was tailed by Linda, whose expression displayed both concern and disapproval.

"It was an accident," she said shakily. "I lost my grip and..." She drifted off, hating the pleading tinge to her voice. "It won't happen again." Why did it feel like that was her new motto?

"Damn right it won't happen again," Henderson snapped back. "You're fired."

She stumbled backwards. "What? You're firing me because I dropped a tray?"

Henderson's features hardened. "I'm firing you because you've displayed some inappropriate behavior as of late, according to Linda." He lifted his hand to tick off each angry point with his fingers. "You changed the weekly schedule to suit your own personal needs." He lifted another finger. "There was a complaint made about you." Another finger. "You were late for work." Another finger. "And you just caused a scene in front of a room full of customers. Clean out your locker, Ms. Reilly."

"Mr. Henderson—"

"Don't argue with me. The bar has already been getting bad reviews, and the scene out there did not help the Olive Martini's reputation. You no longer work for this establishment, Ms. Reilly. Is that understood?"

She blinked back the hot tears prickling her eyes. "It's understood," she finally muttered.

"Good. Now *clean out your locker.*"

It was only ten o'clock when Ben let himself into Maggie's apartment with the key she'd given him in the cab. He'd gone back to his brownstone to pick up some clothes, but when he'd found a lone reporter lurking on the curb he quickly hopped in a cab and headed right back to Maggie's. He hadn't expected her to be home from work until later, so he was surprised to walk in and find her sitting on the couch. Even more surprised at the sight of her puffy red eyes and tear-stained cheeks.

In a flash, he crossed the room and dropped next to her on the couch.

"Hey, don't cry," he said roughly, pulling her into his arms. "It's okay."

"It's not okay." She gulped and then eased out of his embrace. "I got fired tonight."

"What?"

"The owner of the bar fired me."

Ben grew silent, a wave of uneasiness climbing up his chest. He couldn't imagine why a dedicated worker like Maggie would ever be canned. His throat tightened at the memory of how he'd gone behind her back to cancel her shift, and he wondered if maybe that had something to do with it. Oh Christ, had he gotten her fired?

"Maggie..." He bit the inside of his cheek. "I have something I need to tell you."

She pinned him down with a hard look. "I already know. You got Trisha to take my shift. Don't worry, your little trick wasn't the only reason I was let go." She snorted. "I've been late a couple times. Oh, and I dropped a tray."

He faltered. "You dropped a tray."

"Yep. Broke a couple of glasses, spilled some beer on the floor."

"You were fired for *that*?"

"To quote the owner, I 'caused a scene'."

"That son of a bitch."

She gave a small sniffle, and more tears welled up in her eyes and coated her thick lashes. "That son of a bitch was signing my paychecks. And now..." The tears overflowed and

189

slid down her cheeks.

"Now what?"

The look she gave him made his heart ache. "Now I can't pay off the rest of my tuition. I still owe the college for this semester."

"I'll pay it." The words flew out before he could stop them.

"You're not paying my bills." She swiped at her eyes with the sleeve of her sweater. "I'll figure out a way. Maybe the bank will give me a loan."

"Let me handle it."

He was begging now, but he didn't care. He couldn't just stand by and do nothing when she looked at him with so much pain in her eyes. He couldn't stand by and watch her cry.

"No, Ben."

"Goddammit, Maggie, just let me take care of you."

She didn't answer.

"You can't do it, can you? You can't let anyone else carry some of your burden." He exhaled slowly. "Why the hell won't you let me help you? Why won't you let me in?"

Rather than answering the question, she just wiped her eyes again and frowned. Myriad emotions flickered in her eyes, anger and confusion the most dominant, but rather than say whatever what was on her mind, her face became expressionless and she stumbled to her feet. "I don't want to talk about this anymore," she burst out. "I need a hot shower." Without another word, she left the room.

Maggie closed her eyes and let the warm water slide over her face, easing the ache in her swollen eyes. She couldn't remember the last time she'd cried. To her, tears had always been a sign of weakness, vulnerability. She hadn't felt vulnerable since she was child, and it bothered her that she was crying over losing her job. People lost their jobs all the time, it was a trivial fact of life. It wasn't the end of the world.

Only it wasn't trivial to her. Her job at the Olive paid her bills. Her savings were nonexistent, and with exams coming up it wasn't likely she could find another job in time to pay the rest of her tuition. She was already accruing late fees like crazy, since she hadn't paid the amount in full at the beginning of the year like most students. Without her job, how could she pay the college?

She shut off the water and stepped out of the shower. Wrapping a terry-cloth robe over herself, she belted it tightly and reached for the door handle, but paused before turning it, wondering if Ben was still out in the living room. Wondering if he'd start needling her again about letting him help her.

God, she didn't want him to help her. And besides, a part of her was still so bitter about his involvement in her firing. Why the hell had he gone behind her back and messed around with her work schedule? How had he convinced her to leave town for two days? Why couldn't he just go away?

You don't want him to go away.

She ignored that taunting little voice in her head, telling herself that of course she wanted him to leave. Tonight proved that he was a complication, a distraction she couldn't afford. He might have given her the best sex of her life, but was it worth all the headaches? The reporters who surrounded them in the airport? The loss of her job?

No, it wasn't worth it at all. She'd worked too hard to have all her goals threatened by a damn movie star.

She strode out of the bathroom, determined to tell Ben it was over. That it was time for him to face the press. Time to stop using her as an excuse to hide out. Time to *un*complicate

Elle Kennedy

her life. But when she entered the bedroom and found him sitting on the bed, the speech she'd prepared died on her lips.

He looked so damn upset that her chest squeezed a little. His broad shoulders were slumped over, his handsome features creased with worry, and when he looked up at her approach, the remorse flickering in his cobalt blue eyes was unmistakable.

He stood up and said, "I'm sorry."

"Ben—"

"No, listen to me." He stepped closer and touched her chin with one warm hand. "I'm really sorry about the way I fucked everything up. I'm sorry about those reporters at the airport, and I'm *really* sorry I tricked you into going to the Bahamas with me."

"Ben—"

He cut her off with a kiss, his lips softer and gentler than they'd ever been. She tried to focus, tried to tell him that it was time they parted ways, but the feel of his hot mouth on hers was too distracting. Seeing as she'd just lost her job, the last thing she should want to do was have sex, but her body instantly responded to Ben.

"Let me make it up to you," he murmured into her mouth.

She wanted to argue, wanted to tell him the only way to make it up to her was to leave, to take his complications elsewhere and let her work it out on her own, but her desire for him was too damn strong.

One last time, a little voice pleaded inside her head.

She shouldn't listen to that voice, she knew that. Falling into bed with Ben, even if it was just one last time, wouldn't make the situation any better. She still wouldn't have her job, the press would still be sniffing around her, Ben would still be asking her for things she wasn't sure she could give. Sex wasn't going to change that.

Yet she couldn't ignore her body's need for this man. And when his blue eyes locked with hers and asked an unspoken question, she couldn't seem to say no.

So she nodded.

Without another word, Ben led her toward the bed and slowly peeled the robe off her body. Then he lay her down on the patterned bedspread and kissed her again. He kissed everywhere. Her lips. Her nipples. Her stomach, her thighs, her clit.

As his tongue dragged across every inch of her, all the events of the night dissolved and fled her body in the form of a soft whimper.

Silently, Ben removed his own clothes and lowered his body on hers.

Their gazes collided, and what she saw in his blue eyes stole the breath from her lungs. He looked turned on and contented and even a little vulnerable, which made her heart do flip-flops in her chest.

"Maggie," he finally said, his voice coming out hoarse, ragged.

She waited for him to continue. He didn't. Instead he started to move inside her, his pace a languid rolling rhythm that had her gasping with impatience. He ignored her tiny whimpers, the way she gripped his buttocks and tried to pull him deeper inside her.

"There's no rush," he whispered, pushing strands of hair out of her eyes.

He resumed the slow pace and she wasn't sure how long they lay there, how long he rocked inside her and made love to her. Minutes could have ticked by, hours even, but Maggie didn't care. Her eyelids fluttered, then closed, and she almost purred, breathing in Ben's spicy masculine scent.

She kissed his chest, running her tongue along his collarbone, meeting his gentle thrusts with the measured rise of her hips. And just when she thought she'd pass out from ecstasy, he withdrew his shaft and slid down between her legs, pressing his lips to her swollen clit. Licking, sucking, until she cried out from an orgasm so intense a wave of dizziness crashed over her.

Ben didn't let her recover, nor did he resume his lazy pace when he slid back inside her. "Now we can rush," he muttered, thrusting into her so fast and so hard that an astonishing second orgasm seized her inner muscles.

She cried out again. Stunned, unprepared for that second explosion of pleasure. A moment later, Ben shuddered and came, finally allowing himself his own release.

He kissed her forehead, and then gently rolled off her to dispose of the condom. Staring at his sinewy, sweat-soaked back, Maggie bit her lip to stop herself from asking him what just happened. Sex happened, yes, but something between them had shifted. Something that scared her, yet exhilarated her at the same time. Something she couldn't explain with words, or label, or even analyze.

And for the first time in her life, Maggie wondered if that something might just be love.

Chapter Twelve

Maggie didn't wake him before she slid out of the apartment the next morning. She knew it made her a coward, knew she should've woken Ben, maybe even talked about what happened between them last night, but she wasn't ready to face any of it yet. Something had changed last night and she knew he'd felt it too. It showed in the way he'd held her after sex, the way he'd tenderly stroked her hair and fallen asleep with his head against her breasts. The entire exchange had been so damn intimate that she didn't even know what to make of it. It worried her. So much that she was leaving the apartment without a word and heading to the community center despite the chicken pox risk.

She just couldn't be around Ben right now. Last night, when the L-word had floated its way into her head, she'd been stunned. And scared. Really scared.

She'd never been in love before, never allowed herself to feel anything even remotely close to it, and that she'd somehow dropped her guard around Ben was terrifying. She was supposed to hate him for messing around with her job, for complicating her entire life with his sexy smiles and drugging kisses.

So why didn't she hate him, damn it?

A day working with the kids was what she needed. Sundays

weren't usually her days to volunteer, but she needed to be out of the apartment, away from Ben and the conflicting emotions he stirred inside her. For some reason, kids always had the strangest ability to clear your head and help you gain perspective on life.

Paying the cab driver, she stepped out of the car and onto the sidewalk. The temperature was surprisingly hot for May, the sky a clear blue and the breeze warm as it snaked through her hair. Yet, in spite of such a perfect New York City day, an ominous cloud hung in the air.

As she neared the community center, the cloud thickened, bringing a chill to her body and making her stop in her tracks. There was a crowd milling in front of the Broger Center. Not just a crowd, but a crowd with cameras and microphones and news vans. A crowd that rushed toward her the second she walked up.

"Maggie!" one reporter shouted.

Oh God.

"Ms. Reilly, how long have you been seeing Ben Barrett?"

"Are you aware of his affair with Gretchen Goodrich?"

She wanted to melt into the sidewalk and become one with the cement, but the press wouldn't let her. Before she could blink, they'd surrounded her. Stuck microphones in her face. Grinned at her like a pack of hyenas about to devour a carcass. *Her* carcass.

"Maggie, did Mr. Barrett pay you for sex? Is that why you were with him at the Lester Hotel?"

Something very sharp pierced her heart. They were implying she was a *prostitute*?

Unable to breathe, she pushed one of the microphones out of her face and stalked forward. "I won't even dignify that with an answer," she spat.

She zigzagged through the mob, her steps getting faster and faster the closer she got to the door. Once inside the community center, she hurried down the corridor and waited until she was out of sight from the front windows before she sagged against the wall and gasped for air.

Why the hell was this happening to her? Why did these strangers even care about her?

"Maggie?"

She lifted her head and saw one of the counselors eyeing her with concern. "Hi, Karen," she said, her voice unsteady.

"Gloria is in her office." Karen looked hesitant. "You should probably go in and see her."

"All right."

Collecting her nerves, she walked toward the main office and stepped inside. The counselor who doubled as a receptionist greeted her with a sympathetic smile. An omen of things to come, obviously.

She headed for the center facilitator's open doorway. The tiny Hispanic woman behind the desk gestured for her to close the door then said, "Have a seat."

Maggie sat. Waiting.

"Apparently you're something of a celebrity." Gloria's tone wasn't angry, but mild. Her gaze not accusatory, but concerned.

"Gloria...I'm so sorry about all this."

She wrung her hands together, laced her fingers, then unlaced them, then tucked her palms on her knees, but no amount of fidgeting could stop the river of guilt flowing inside her. Damn it. The kids at the center didn't deserve to have a bunch of slimy reporters snapping their pictures. Nobody here deserved all this unwanted attention.

"So you're dating a movie star," Gloria continued, offering a small smile. "To be honest, I'm not sure I envy you or pity you. Having the media on your back must be awful."

She gulped. "Yes, it is."

"Maggie, I'm going to be honest here. All this attention isn't good for the center."

A sigh lodged in the back of her throat. "I know."

"You also know that the reason we try to remain low-key is to protect the families who come here."

Maggie nodded, knowing exactly what Gloria meant. Though the Broger Center, on the surface at least, seemed like every other community center in the city, it also provided shelter for victims of abuse. Women came here to escape from abusive husbands or boyfriends, and the center had a few rooms on the third floor where they could stay until they figured out their next move.

Needless to say, the center wouldn't be a safe haven as long as its picture was splashed all over the papers.

"None of the kids who come here, or their parents, deserve to be pulled into a celebrity scandal." Gloria's voice drew her from her troubled thoughts.

"I agree," she said. "And I promise you I'll straighten all this out."

"I know you will." Gloria leaned forward and rested her elbows on the desk. "But, until you do, it might be a good idea for you not to come in."

Maggie's heart squeezed. "Okay."

"I know you wanted a permanent counseling position here, honey, but right now isn't the time to discuss it. Why don't we let the media storm die down before we talk about anything permanent?"

The facilitator's words were like individual little gunshots. They penetrated her flesh and left a feeling of raw emptiness in Maggie's stomach. Piece by piece, her life crumbled around her. Everything she'd worked so hard for. Everything she'd dreamed of achieving. Gone.

Losing her job at the Olive was bad. Losing her place at the community center absolutely crushed her.

"I guess I'll be in touch then," she murmured, fighting hard to stop the tears prickling her eyelids from spilling over. She rose to her feet and extended her hand. "Thanks for being so nice about this."

Gloria shook her hand. "This isn't personal, honey. I'm just trying to protect our kids and their parents. Give me a call when things settle down, okay?"

"Sure."

She left Gloria's office with her chin high and her shoulders stiff, but it took all her willpower not to collapse on the linoleum floor beneath her feet. Somehow her legs managed to carry her outside, where she pushed through the reporters and uttered the words "no comment" so many times she wanted to scream.

They followed her. Actually followed her to the curb, hurling questions at her. Ben Barrett. Gretchen Goodrich. Lester Hotel. Sex. Affair. The words all mingled into one pounding bassline, making her head hurt and her stomach churn.

Only when she flagged down a cab and slid into the backseat did she finally allow the tears to fall.

Ben already knew about the reporters at the center when Maggie walked into the apartment. He'd seen it on the news, and he'd never felt so powerless as the segment flashed across the screen. Never felt so enraged when he'd seen Maggie's wide, confused eyes and the expression of sheer shock she'd donned when that one reporter asked if Ben had paid her for sex.

The accusation left him sick to his stomach. Getting paid for sex? Maggie did *not* deserve to be humiliated like that, and on national television no less.

"Mags," he started as she dropped her keys on the hall table and silently headed for the kitchen.

He followed her, uneasy, maybe even a bit scared as he watched her open the cupboard under the sink and rummage around. She pulled out a bottle of Jamaican rum and twisted off the cap.

"Maggie..."

Still no answer. Face blank, she found a pink plastic cup, poured the dark liquid into it and lifted the cup to her lips.

"Goddammit, Maggie, will you talk to me?"

Her throat bobbed as she swallowed, her face scrunched up in disgust. "God, no wonder I don't drink. This tastes awful."

She turned around and dumped the contents of the cup into the sink, then returned the liquor bottle to its place in the cupboard.

"They followed me home," she said, crossing her arms over her chest. "They're outside the building."

Ben's features creased with frustration. "I'll call my agent and publicist to see how we can get rid of them."

"Don't bother."

She blew past him and settled on the living room couch, leaving him to stare after her in bewilderment. Why was she acting so calm? Her privacy was being violated, her good name threatened, and she was lounging around on the sofa?

He rubbed his temples, unnerved by her reaction. He didn't like this. Didn't like that vacant look in her green eyes or the way she was brushing all this off.

"I won't let them say those things about you," he finally burst out. He began to pace the hardwood floor, fists clenched, breath ragged. "We need to put a stop to this."

"Do you love me, Ben?"

He froze.

"Do you love me?" she repeated.

He moistened his dry lips and swept his gaze over her. She looked young and vulnerable in her snug blue jeans and V-neck green T-shirt, her face free of makeup, her delicate features imploring. She'd worn her hair loose today, and it fell down her shoulders in soft waves, straight and curly at the same time, wild and guarded, just like Maggie.

Did he love her? He sure as hell did.

"Ben?"

"Yes, I love you," he said in a rough voice, moving toward her.

"Good." She tucked a strand of hair behind her ear and their eyes locked. "Then you need to leave."

He stumbled back. "What?"

"You need to leave, Ben. If you leave, they leave."

He couldn't believe she was saying this. Yes, his presence in her life was currently causing an enormous mess, but he could make it go away. He was Ben Barrett, for chrissake.

That's the problem, pal.

He tried to push that harsh voice out of his brain, but it wouldn't go away. It wouldn't go away because it was right. *Maggie* was right. The problem here wasn't whether he could get the press to leave her alone, it was that he'd placed her in

201

the spotlight to begin with. His celebrity was costing her so damn much.

If Ben Barrett hadn't been *the* Ben Barrett, but just a normal man with a normal life, Maggie wouldn't be suffering right now.

"Gloria asked me not to come back to the center."

Her soft voice sliced through his disconcerting thoughts. "Because of the press?" he sighed.

"Yep." She paused. "Look, I can find another waitressing job easily, but I can't be a counselor if I'm being followed by reporters. It's not fair to the kids I work with."

"Maybe you can put social work on hold for a while? Just until this all dies down." He almost cringed at the desperation in his tone.

"On hold?" She cast a withering look in his direction. "It's taken me seven years to earn this degree. Attending classes part-time so I could work to pay my tuition. I've sacrificed friendships and relationships in order to keep up my schedule. I don't have a goddamn life because of it, and now you're telling me to put it on hold? That would be like saying all those years of hard work meant absolutely nothing."

"I know."

"I won't throw it all away."

"I know."

His throat tightened to the point where swallowing actually hurt. He knew she was right. He just didn't *want* her to be right.

"I don't fit into your life, Ben. You said so yourself—you live in a plastic world." She rose to her feet and eliminated the distance between them. "I can't live in a plastic world. I need my life to mean something. Especially since I felt so meaningless growing up."

She reached up and stroked his stubble-covered cheek. He hadn't shaved since they'd returned from the Bahamas and the feel of her fingertips scraping over his two-day-old beard was torture.

"You need to leave," she said again.

How perfectly ironic. He'd starred in dozens of movies where he always played the savior and always got the girl, yet in real life it was the exact opposite. He wouldn't get the girl this time. And instead of saving her, he'd turned her entire world off-kilter.

"If you want me to go, I'll go." He choked on the bittersweet lump in his throat. "But I want to thank you first."

"For what?"

"For being so damn real."

Her bottom lip trembled. She blinked a couple times as if fighting back tears. Somehow this made him feel slightly better, knowing that saying goodbye was as hard for her as it was for him. With a small smile, he traced the seam of her lips with his thumb, then lowered his head to kiss the trembling away. It was the slowest kiss they'd ever shared, the softest one, and something inside him shattered when he finally pulled his lips away.

The thought of walking into Maggie's bedroom and gathering the items of clothing he'd brought over was too damn distressing, so he simply took a step back toward the door. He glanced at her over his shoulder, shot her his best Ben Barrett grin, and hoped she couldn't hear the sound of his heart cracking open in his chest.

"Ben?"

He stopped. "Yeah?"

"I'm sorry."

"Don't be. I'm the one who should be sorry." He gripped the door knob with one unsteady hand. "Goodbye, Red."

"The prodigal son returns!" Miranda Barrett chirped as Ben trudged into the front hallway of his childhood home.

It was nearly one in the morning, but somehow Ben wasn't surprised to see his mother up and about. She was the ultimate night owl, and Ben couldn't even count how many times he'd slithered into the house at three in the morning thinking he'd orchestrated a successful sneak-out, only to find his mother baking cookies in the kitchen.

In fact, as he kicked off his shoes and walked toward her, the scent of baked goods floated into his nostrils. His mom's long red apron and the white flour sticking to her gray-streaked hair confirmed that she'd been baking up a storm prior to his arrival.

"You should have told me you were coming to visit," Miranda chided with a shake of her head. "I would've baked another batch."

As a half-smile reached his lips, Ben removed his leather jacket and tossed it aside, then stepped forward to embrace his mother. He kissed the top of her head, and then linked his arm through hers and they strolled through the oak swivel door leading into the kitchen. After receiving his very first million-dollar paycheck, he'd offered to buy his mother a new house, but she'd refused. She loved the small bungalow she'd raised Ben in, and he had to admit he liked it too. It represented a warmth and coziness his life lacked these days.

"I know I should have called," he said as he rounded the counter and flopped onto one of the tall white stools. "Coming here was sort of a last-minute decision."

"Every decision you make is last-minute, Benjamin. You're nothing if not spontaneous."

Well, she had him on that one. His spontaneity was how he'd ended up with Maggie, how he'd forced his way into her apartment—and her life—without even knowing why he was doing it. Look how that turned out, though. He'd fallen in love, sure, but he'd also cost Maggie her job, her dreams and her privacy.

So much for being spontaneous.

"So, what have you done?" Miranda asked as she poured a tall glass of milk and set it on the splintered cedar counter in front of him.

"What makes you think I did something?"

She chuckled, then slid two fluffy oven mitts on her hands and removed a tray of chocolate chip cookies from the oven rack. "You've got guilt written all over your face," she tossed over her shoulder, setting the baking tray on the stove to cool. "And please don't tell me you got another tattoo. One is enough."

"No tattoos." He released the sigh lodged in his chest. "I fell in love, Mom."

The kitchen went so silent you could hear not one, but thirty pins drop on the tiled floor. Gaping, his mother turned to face him.

"Seriously?"

He nodded glumly. "Seriously."

After another second of bewilderment, his mother's dark blue eyes lit up like a string of Christmas lights. She whipped off her oven mitts, marched over, and rested her palms on the counter. "Tell me everything," she ordered with a huge grin.

He told her. About Maggie. About the hotel room mishap that threw them together (though he did leave out the details of what happened *during* that room mishap). He finished with the entire paparazzi mess and Maggie's request that he leave, ending with, "So basically, I screwed up her life."

He let out a groan and reached for the milk in front of him, feeling like a little kid again as he sipped the cold liquid.

"You didn't screw up her life," Miranda soothed. "It will all settle down sooner or later."

"Yeah, until the next scandal hits the newsstands." He tightened his grip on his glass, then, fearing it would shatter, set it down gently. "Maggie doesn't want to be part of my lifestyle, Mom. She doesn't want that kind of attention."

Miranda assumed that knowing look of wisdom he'd grown used to over the years. "The only reason you receive that kind of attention, Benjamin, is because you go out looking for it."

"I certainly do not."

"Sure you do." She shrugged at his indignant frown. "You date floozies, my dear son. And when you date floozies, the media likes to take pictures of you with your floozies."

"Stop saying floozies," he grumbled.

"Don't sulk, sweetheart. You know I'm right."

Fine, so maybe his mother had a point. There were plenty of other celebrities, actors far more famous than him, who didn't find their faces splashed across the tabloids every week. Ben didn't go out and solicit the media's attention, but he could see his mom's point. The women he dated were gorgeous, flashy, demanding to be noticed. Like Sonja, who ought to be wearing a sign that said "notice me, take my picture".

"This Maggie sounds very down to earth," his mother added. "And I don't mean this as an insult, but she also seems like the type who wouldn't make the media drool. They need teeny-bikini models to sell covers, not your average Jane type. She's too normal for those jerks."

Ben smiled. "You're right about that." His expression quickly sobered. "But that doesn't take away from the fact that they're still all over me. Especially ever since Gretchen died."

He almost flinched, expecting to see sorrow—and maybe a bit of anger—in his mother's eyes, but she surprised him. Looking serious, she crossed her arms over her apron and said, "Tell the truth already, Benjamin. Tell them about Gretchen and your father."

His eyebrows shot up. "I'd never do anything to embarrass you, Mom."

Miranda rolled her eyes. "You're embarrassing me now, for God's sake! Everyone in town thinks my son goes to bed with women twice his age. The other day, Susan pulled me aside in the drugstore and suggested you go into therapy."

Ben couldn't help but laugh. "You're lying."

"I certainly am not! Call Susan yourself. I'm sure she has a list of therapists written up."

"So you honestly don't care if I tell the world Dad was a bigamist and a thief?"

"Of course not." Her aristocratic features softened. "Ben, I've come to terms with what your father did. In fact, I came to terms with it a long time ago. You don't need to protect me from it."

"What about the money?"

"What about it?"

"I don't feel right keeping it," he confessed.

"Then give it away." His mother shrugged. "There are a lot of deserving charities out there, and if Gretchen's money is that much of a burden for you, donate it."

Ben reached for his glass again, draining it. As usual, his mother was nothing if not frank. She'd always been frank. Always been the strongest woman he'd ever known, too, which made him wonder why he'd ever believed she'd be embarrassed or ashamed if the truth about his connection to Gretchen came out.

"Now, about this Maggie," Miranda continued, strolling back to the stove to pluck one cookie from the tray. She nibbled on the edge of the cookie, her eyes narrowed. "I assume you'll do everything you can to get her back?"

A smile played on his lips. "You assume right."

"Good." With a brisk nod, she finished chewing and wiped her hands on the front of her apron. "Before I give you a cookie, Benjamin, you've got to tell me one thing."

"Sure."

"Does Maggie have any tattoos?"

His smile widened into a full-blown grin. "Don't worry, she doesn't."

"Thank the lord!" Miranda made a tsking sound with her tongue. "At least one of you has some good sense."

Chapter Thirteen

Two days after she'd sent Ben away, Maggie still hadn't mastered the art of getting off the living room couch and changing out of her ratty old sweats. Tough. She didn't feel like getting up, or brushing her hair, or pretending that she was anything but what she currently felt—miserable.

It's not like she had a job to go to, anyway. No school either, since her first exam wasn't until next week. And though most of the reporters had abandoned their stakeout of the Broger Center, a few overly ambitious ones still lingered, making her feel uneasy about going back. Sooner or later she'd call Gloria and talk about that permanent position.

"Jeez, Maggie, did you rob a bank?" came her roommate's incredulous cry.

Maggie twisted her head in time to see Summer walk through the front door, looking tanned, healthy and seriously confused. In comparison, Maggie felt like a big mess with her tangled hair and wrinkled clothing. A big, pathetic mess.

"Yes, Summer, I robbed a bank," she said dryly.

After staring wide-eyed at her disheveled appearance, Summer dropped the bright red suitcase she held in her hands and marched toward the couch. "Seriously, why are there reporters standing outside our building? I heard one of them quizzing the security guard about you. Are you in trouble?"

"I guess you could say that." She released a sigh that drained her entire chest of oxygen. "I did something stupid."

"Oh God, do I want to know?"

"I fell in love with a movie star."

Summer's stunned silence didn't come as any surprise. Hell, she'd been pretty damn stunned herself when she'd first figured it out. After Ben left, she'd been understandably upset. She'd lost her job, her position at the center, her dream of a successful career. And yet when she'd gone to bed alone that first evening, something shocking happened.

Lying there in bed, staring up at the dark ceiling, she'd come to a realization that left any chance of falling asleep absolutely impossible.

She'd realized that the ache in her heart, the empty feeling in her stomach, that unbearable weight bearing down on her chest, had nothing to do with losing her job.

And everything to do with losing Ben.

"How long have I been gone for?" Summer said, blinking wildly. "In a week and a half you managed to fall in love with a movie star? Is this a joke?"

"No, it's true."

Summer motioned for her to move over, and then flopped down next to her on the couch. "Okay, spill."

"Remember my stranger?"

"Of course."

"Turns out he's Ben Barrett, the celebrity I was asking you about at the Olive, where I'm no longer employed, by the way."

"Why the hell not?"

"It's a long story."

"Try me."

"Just remember, you asked for it." In a shaky voice, Maggie recapped all the events of the past week and a half.

"Holy shit," Summer breathed when she finished. "I'm so sorry, Maggie."

"Don't be sorry." Her hand trembled as she waved it dismissively. "You didn't cause any of this."

Summer opened her mouth to reply, but the ring of the telephone cut her off. Shooting her roommate a pleading look, Maggie handed her the cordless phone.

"Hello?" Summer said into the receiver. She paused, then handed the phone back. "It's for you."

A tiny pang of hope tugged at her insides, but she willed it away. It wouldn't be Ben. She'd asked him to leave. He hadn't called since and he wouldn't call now.

She was right.

"Maggie, it's Tony."

The weight returned to her chest, heavier this time, stifling. "Hi, Tony."

"I've got good news, babe. I'll be in the city tomorrow night."

He'd be in the city? She almost laughed out loud, realizing how things had changed so astronomically since the last time she'd spoken to—or thought about—Tony. A few weeks ago she'd have jumped up and down with excitement at the sound of his voice, at the idea of meeting up with Tony and going to bed with him. Now, it was the last thing she wanted.

How could she just forget about everything that happened and go back the way she was in the pre-Ben days? How could she ever settle for casual sex when she'd experienced something deeper?

"That's great," she finally answered, her tone hardly enthusiastic.

Elle Kennedy

"Don't sound so thrilled about it," he teased.

"I'm sorry. I just...I've met someone." Next to her, Summer's eyebrows shot up to her hairline.

There was a brief silence. "You're kidding me," Tony finally said with a laugh.

"It's not funny, you know."

"I'm not making fun of you, hon. I'm just stunned. What happened to the Maggie I meet three times a year?"

"Two times," she corrected.

Tony sounded perplexed. "Is it serious?"

She drew in a breath. "Yeah. I think so. I'm sorry, Tony."

"Hey, don't apologize. We had a good run, don't ya think?"

"It was great," she said, and she meant it. It *had* been great, the casual trysts with Tony. But she didn't want great anymore. She wanted incredible. She wanted body-numbing. Toe-curling. Heart-thumping.

She wanted Ben.

Feeling her eyes well up with unwelcome tears, she said a quick goodbye and hung up, swiping at her damp lashes with the sleeve of her sweatshirt. Damn it. She was sick of crying.

Lifting her chin, she ran her hands through her messy hair and released a groan. "This is why I never wanted anything serious. Feeling miserable sucks."

Summer stared at her. "You're a different person. How the hell did this happen?"

She managed a faint smile. "Shocking, huh?"

"No, I'm serious, Mags." Summer rubbed her temples. "You just broke it off with Tony. Tony, for God's sake! The guy you can't wait to see each time he comes to visit."

"I guess Two-Time Tony isn't enough anymore," she finally

admitted. "Ben...well, he made me realize something."

"You've already fallen for the guy," Summer teased. "What more could you have realized?"

"That I don't want to be alone."

Instantly the anvil pressing down on her ribcage lifted. Saying the words out loud was difficult but cathartic because they were so undeniably true. The past couple days without Ben had been horrible. Miserable and horrible and excruciatingly lonely.

The loneliness was what finally got to her. For so long she'd worked her ass off to make *something* of herself. She'd wanted her life to mean something, she'd wanted to matter, if only to the kids she worked with, and that's what always drove her. Saving money, getting a college degree, finding a meaningful job. But what happened afterwards? What happened when she went home at night, alone? When she woke up every morning, alone? When the only person she was able to share her dreams, thoughts and feelings with was a roommate who'd soon be building her own life with the man she loved?

So she would have a career, so she'd spend her afternoons doing something meaningful, but what was the point if she didn't have anyone to share it with?

"I miss him," she finally admitted. "I miss talking to him, and joking around with him. I miss kissing him. Hell, I even miss listening to him sing along to the Beach Boys."

A knowing smile curved Summer's mouth. "It's a pretty amazing feeling, isn't it? Being in love?" She paused. "Listen, I know this probably isn't the time to tell you this, but...Tygue and I are getting married."

For a moment, all of Maggie's problems whisked out of her tired brain. "Really?"

Summer blushed prettily. "He proposed on the last night of

our trip. We're thinking a Christmas wedding in Jamaica."

"I'm happy for you, Summer."

"Thanks." She paused again. "Why don't you call him?"

"Tygue? I can just congratulate him in person."

"Not Tygue. Ben."

"I can't call him."

"Why not?"

"Because I asked him to leave."

"So ask him to come back."

Maggie swallowed. "It's not that simple. Look, even if I do tell him how I feel, the media won't stop harassing us. And as long as reporters are interested in me, Gloria won't let me work at the center."

Summer's expression softened. "Then you need to ask yourself this—what's more important to you, your job or the man you love?"

"C'mon, Summer, don't make this about me having to choose."

"What if that's what it comes down to?"

Maggie grew silent. What if it *did* come to that? She wasn't sure what she'd do if that happened. She wanted to be with Ben, but she wasn't ready to give up everything she'd worked so hard for either.

And what if she did decide Ben was worth being hounded by the paparazzi, worth risking her job for? If they ended up breaking up someday, she'd be left with nothing. She'd be no better than her mother, a woman who'd left her responsibilities on a sidewalk in Queens for a man and a relationship that— knowing her mother's flakiness—probably hadn't even worked out.

Did her mom regret leaving her? It wasn't the first time she'd wondered, and it probably wouldn't be the last, but it was the question that always kept her in line, always urged her to make something of herself.

Because if she did get Ben back, and if it didn't end up working out, the last thing she wanted was to be left with regrets.

"I don't want to talk about this right now," she finally blurted, too confused to think. "Tell me about your trip. How did the steel drum performance go? Did you get along with Tygue's family?"

As if sensing Maggie had officially dropped the subject of love and Ben Barrett, Summer finally sighed. Then she smiled. "Actually, his family loved me. *And* everyone at the reception gave me a standing ovation after I finished my song."

"Now that I've got to see to believe."

"Don't you worry, Doubting Maggie. Luckily for you, Tygue got it all on video..."

"Ben, have a seat," Alan Goodrich said after the two men had entered the spacious living room of Goodrich's ten-bedroom mansion in Beverly Hills.

Ben assumed a relaxed demeanor and sank onto the plush black leather sofa situated in front of a forbidding stone fireplace. He'd visited the Goodrich home only once before, when Gretchen first contacted him six months ago, but the luxurious surroundings still made him a little uncomfortable. Hell, being in Alan's presence made him uncomfortable. The man was one of the most esteemed directors in the business, recipient of two Oscars, not to mention a list of nominations and critic nods as long as the Nile.

215

He still wasn't sure why Alan wanted to meet with him, but he hoped it didn't have to do with Gretchen.

Of course it has to do with Gretchen, his brain argued. *Why else did he ask you to come?*

"I have two matters to discuss with you," Alan announced.

"Okay," Ben said, slightly unnerved.

With his big, beefy body, a head of white hair and piercing green eyes, Alan Goodrich was nothing if not intimidating. Lowering his body into a leather recliner, Alan folded his hands in his lap. "First, you should know that my wife's estate has been settled. Since the will was uncontested, you should receive a check very soon."

Ben swallowed. "About that...I don't feel comfortable keeping Gretchen's money, Mr. Goodrich."

"Call me Alan."

"Okay. Alan. Well, I've decided to donate the money to charity." When Goodrich didn't object, Ben went on. "I also wanted to ask you something. I'd like to give a statement to the press, about Gretchen's connection to my father."

Alan grew silent.

"That is, if you don't mind," he added quickly.

"Actually, I think it's a fine idea." Goodrich's strong, somewhat harsh features softened. "Gretchen would've hated it if she knew your inheritance caused a media circus. She really did feel awful about what your father did to you and your mother. I don't think she would've ever written you into her will if she knew the kind of negative attention you'd receive."

"I know."

"So clear it up, son. It's about time the press cut you some slack."

"Thanks, Alan."

Goodrich gave a brisk nod. "Now, the second matter at hand. I don't know if you've heard, but I'm currently working on a war epic."

"I'd heard, yes."

"I've just approved the screenplay, and we're scouting locations and beginning to cast as we speak."

Ben crossed his ankles together, suddenly remembering the words Maggie had said to him in the Bahamas. *Nobody's going to give it to you. If you want something, you go after it.*

He wasn't sure where Goodrich was heading or why he'd mentioned his latest film, but Ben knew he couldn't allow the opportunity to slip through his fingers. Maggie was right. He couldn't sit around and wait for a meaty role to fall into his lap. If he wanted it, he needed to go out and get it.

"About your film..." he ventured quietly. "I was actually going to ask you if you'd let me read for it."

Goodrich chuckled. "Ben—"

He tried not to bristle at the director's laughter and hurried on. "I'm not asking for a leading role, Alan. I'll read for any part you want, as small as you want."

"Ben—"

"Just give me a shot."

"That's exactly what I intend to do," Alan said, chuckling again. "If you had let me finish, you would have heard me offering you one of the supporting roles."

His jaw fell open despite his attempt to keep it shut. "Pardon me?"

Alan offered a faint smile. "Don't look so shocked. I've told you before how much I enjoy your screen performances."

"Yeah, but I thought..." he trailed off.

"You thought I was bullshitting?" Alan finished, his smile

widening. "I wasn't. You truly are a fine actor, son. And the moment I finished reading the script, I knew I wanted you to be in the film."

Before Ben could answer, a mechanical rendition of a Beethoven symphony broke out. With an apologetic look, Goodrich reached into the inner pocket of the navy-blue blazer he wore and extracted a cell phone. "I need to take this."

As the director stood up and exited the room, Ben rubbed his forehead, still a little stunned. Alan Goodrich had just offered him a role in his new movie? Sure, there was bound to be action in the war epic, the gunfire and explosions he'd grown used to, but there would also be depth to it. Not to mention the respect and prestige working with a director of Alan's caliber provided. Just having his name attached to an Alan Goodrich project would certainly make the critics take him seriously, even if he was Bad Boy Ben Barrett.

Hell, with all that recognition, maybe the media would finally drop the alliteration-heavy nickname and see him as simply Ben Barrett, actor.

"I'm going to have to cut this meeting short," came Goodrich's rueful voice.

Ben turned to see the director standing in the doorway, still holding his cell phone. Getting to his feet, he walked toward Alan and extended his hand. "Not a problem. I've got somewhere to be anyway."

Alan gave his hand a firm shake. "I'll be in touch about the film. We'll probably start shooting at the end of the summer. Sound good?"

"Sounds great."

Ben left the Goodrich estate feeling like he was walking on air. During the past half hour an enormous weight had lifted off his chest, the weight of discontent and frustration over a career that had strayed off in a direction Ben had never wanted. But it was back on track again, and soon the other pieces of his life would fall back into place.

First things first, though. He had a press conference to attend.

Maggie approached the front steps of the Broger Center the next morning and spotted a half dozen reporters milling about, a sight that made her frown. Didn't these people have lives? Homes to go to, kids to take care of? Fortunately she'd finally showered and changed her clothes, but at this point she'd rather look grimy and gross on television than listen to more accusations from the press.

She hadn't slept a wink last night, not when she still missed Ben, not when she was swamped with regret about asking him to leave. After lying in bed until one a.m., she'd finally decided enough was enough. She'd reached for the phone, intending to call Ben, only to realize that she didn't have his damn phone number!

She'd dragged Summer out of bed to help her search the Internet, and though they'd spent hours looking for a contact number, all they got was a fan mail address. And when they'd finally hit pay dirt and learned the name of Ben's agent, it had been too late to call.

Of course, that meant another sleepless night, which only got worse when she rolled her exhausted body out of bed this morning and heard Gloria's voice on her answering machine.

Now, seeing all the reporters on the front steps only made her bad mood a hundred times worse.

"Did you know Ben Barrett was donating his inheritance to the community center?" one of the reporters shouted at her approach.

She stopped for a second. What the hell was this guy talking about?

"Maggie," someone else called. "Were you aware that Ben's father was a bigamist?"

Huh?

Not bothering to respond, she walked into the center and immediately headed for the main office, her head swimming. How did they find out about Ben's father? And what on earth did they mean he'd donated his inheritance to the center?

"Maggie, I'm glad you came in!" Gloria chirped when she entered her office.

The expression on the facilitator's olive-colored face was so jubilant, Maggie's confusion doubled. She sat in the visitor's chair and tried to paste on a cheerful expression. Hard, when she was feeling anything but cheerful.

"I take it the reporters are still harassing everyone," she sighed, avoiding Gloria's eyes.

The older woman waved a dismissive hand. "They'll go away sooner or later."

Maggie's eyebrows shot to her forehead. Had she somehow been transported to a different planet during the night? A few days ago, Gloria had spoken of the media's presence as if it were the anti-Christ. This morning, she seemed unperturbed and relaxed about the entire situation.

"One of the reporters outside mentioned Ben donated some money to the center?" she began, feeling a little awkward about her ignorance on the subject.

Gloria's dark eyes lit up. "Five million dollars is not some money, sweetheart. I'm still overwhelmed by Mr. Barrett's generosity."

Five million dollars?

"I must say, I'm very impressed with the man," Gloria added with a smile. "That he donated half of his recent inheritance to various child service agencies across the country is commendable, but giving the other half to the center? It's unbelievably generous."

"I can't believe he did this," Maggie murmured. Then a frown reached her lips. Ben's gift was so incredible that for a moment she'd forgotten about her last encounter with the woman in front of her. "Gloria, Ben's donation means that the reporters won't be going away for a while..."

Gloria's face softened, remorse reflecting in her gaze. "Maggie, I may have overreacted during our last meeting. My biggest concern at the time was what the attention would do to the center, not to mention how the parents would feel. Turns out most of them are thrilled by the free publicity."

"They are?"

Gloria nodded whole-heartedly. "Many of them feel this will be good for the community, maybe spur the city counselors to take notice of what's happening outside their offices. And now, thanks to Mr. Barrett's generosity, we'll be able to bring about a lot of changes."

Leaning forward, Gloria rested her palms on the desk, her expression growing excited. "His donation will allow us to completely renovate the center, and we're planning on building a new playground and an on-site tutoring center for kids with learning problems."

"What about the shelter?"

"That's the best part. We're going to use a portion of the money to build a women's shelter, in a separate location. More space, more counselors, it'll be wonderful."

Maggie was speechless. Well, considering her last meeting

with Gloria, she hadn't expected the woman to be so pleased about the turn of events.

"So you're okay with the media hanging around?" she asked warily.

"I don't have much of a choice," Gloria replied with a dry smile. "With a donation this size, it's expected. Besides, it really is good publicity, which is something I failed to consider when we spoke last time."

"I'm glad something good came out of all this," Maggie finally said.

"Something great, you mean," Gloria corrected. "I also forgot to mention, we're going to offer after-school workshops for the kids. Drama, music, art. In fact, we've just hired a drama teacher. He'll be working with the kids all summer."

"That's wonderful."

Gloria rose from her chair. "I'd like you to meet him."

She furrowed her brows. "You would?"

Catching her mystified expression, Gloria offered a slight smile. "Humor me, will you?"

Still a bit perplexed, Maggie stood up and followed Gloria out of the small office toward the main corridor. Most of the rooms in the Broger Center were miniscule, but they did have a large indoor gymnasium the kids used during the winter and on rainy days, and Gloria led her in the direction of the gym. They paused in front of the splintered double doors.

"And Maggie, I would like to speak to you afterwards about that permanent position," Gloria added as she reached for the door handle.

Her heart soared. "Really?"

"You're going to make a great counselor, kiddo."

Maggie expected Gloria to enter the gym first, but the

woman simply opened the door and gestured for her to go in.

"You're not coming?" she said in surprise.

"Naah." Gloria gave a small grin. "I already got his autograph."

His autograph?

Baffled, Maggie walked in, and then stopped in her tracks when she laid eyes on Ben.

Clad in a pair of faded blue jeans, a snug black T-shirt and black combat boots, he stood near one of the long wooden benches in front of the boys' locker room. "Hey, Red," he called when he saw her, his deep voice bouncing off the gymnasium walls.

She gulped. God, he looked good. He'd shaved, but his angular face still possessed that hint of bad-boy sexiness, and his perfectly shaped lips looked so damn kissable Maggie shivered. She glanced over her shoulder at Gloria, but the woman had discreetly disappeared, leaving her and Ben alone.

"What are you doing here?" she squeaked.

He crossed the waxed floor with lazy strides, each step he took making her pulse quicken. When he finally stood in front of her, her heart was thudding against her ribs and pounding in her ears.

"I'm going to be teaching a free acting workshop here for the summer," he replied with a charming smile.

"Why?"

He shrugged. "Because I have the summer off. I figured it would be fun."

"I mean, why here?" she stammered. "I'm sure thousands of people would pay big bucks to learn acting from you."

"Haven't you learned by now that I don't care about money?"

Elle Kennedy

She had no idea how to respond. A hundred questions bit at her tongue but she forced herself not to ask them. Quizzing Ben about his donation or his presence here didn't matter right now. Not when they had more important things to say. Not when *she* had something important to say.

"I'm sorry I asked you to leave," she finally whispered.

"You had every right to."

He reached out and stroked her cheek with the pad of his thumb. She held her breath, waiting for him to pull her toward him, anticipating his kiss, but it didn't come. Instead, his features creased with remorse and his hand dropped to his side.

"I made a mess of your life, babe, and I don't blame you for asking me to go." His Adam's apple bobbed. "I knew I couldn't try to get you back until I fixed everything."

"You didn't mess up my life, Ben."

"You lost your job."

"And I got a new one, here at the center." She stepped closer and pressed her palm to his chest. "*And* I figured out quite a few things."

"Like what?"

He covered her hand with his and gently moved it against his heart. She could feel the loud thump-thump of his heartbeat and it brought a smile to her lips, knowing his heart was pounding as hard as hers.

"I figured out it's okay to allow a few complications into my life, that sometimes complicated is better than being alone. Being lonely."

"You're lonely?"

"Ever since you left," she murmured.

"Me too."

He gripped her hand and lifted it to his neck, then reached down and encircled her waist. Twining her arms around him, she leaned up on her tip-toes and brushed her lips over his. "I missed you, Ben."

"I missed you too, Red."

He covered her mouth with a crushing kiss, one of his trademark rough and greedy kisses that left her absolutely breathless. She pushed her tongue into his mouth, wanting more, needing more.

It was Ben who finally broke the kiss, groaning softly in her ear as his obvious erection poked against her navel. "We're in the middle of a children's gymnasium," he muttered, his warm breath fanning over her forehead.

"Then let's go somewhere private. I'm sure the Lester Hotel has a few rooms available," she teased.

Ben shot her his movie star grin. "First we need to get a few things straight."

"I should've known you'd get all demanding on me."

"I'm making it clear, right here and right now, that I'm not leaving you ever again," he said in a stern voice. "If you don't like it, tough."

"I like it," she assured him, fighting a smile. "I'm not going anywhere either."

"Even when the press gets in our faces again?" His cobalt eyes clouded over. "And I do mean *when*, honey. If you choose to stay with me, you'll need to get used to the vultures."

"If being with you means getting my picture taken every now and then, it's a sacrifice I'm willing to make." She quirked her lips. "Like I said, I'm not going anywhere."

He tossed out another hurdle. "Even if I force you to take some time off work and join me in Prague when shooting starts for Alan Goodrich's latest film?"

She gasped. "He gave you a role?"

"Yep. With lines and everything, not just car chases."

"That's great." Her eyes lit up. "I've never been to Prague."

"Well, you can't stay too long," he warned. "My mom is anxious to start all the wedding plans."

Her heart stopped. "Wedding plans?"

"Oh right." He grinned sheepishly. "I forgot, we're getting married."

"That was the worst proposal ever," she complained.

He squeezed her butt and laughed again. "And there it is, that infamous Maggie honesty."

"Get used to it, pal, because I don't sugarcoat anything and you know it."

"That's precisely why I love you."

She slid one hand down his back and gave his butt a squeeze of her own. "I love you too."

He chuckled arrogantly. "Of course you do. I'm Ben Barrett, remember?"

Epilogue

"Ohhh. Oh God. Oh, Ben..."

"Quit acting like a baby," Ben ordered as he clutched Maggie's right hand and squeezed it.

"But it hurts," she shot back.

Greg, the tattoo artist, a man with the build of a pro wrestler and the buzz cut of a Navy SEAL, cast her an apologetic look. "I'm trying to be gentle."

He lowered the needle back to her skin and she could swear she heard her tailbone crack. God, this was awful. She wanted to throttle her husband, but it really wasn't Ben's fault. It had been her brainchild to get a tattoo to celebrate their one-year wedding anniversary.

Husband. Anniversary. It amazed her even thinking the words. Who could have foreseen that one?

"You wanted to do this," Ben reminded her after she let out another soft whimper of pain.

"You could have tried to stop me."

He grinned. "Why would I do that? I think you're going to look hot with a tattoo."

"Your mother is going to kill me."

"She'll get over it."

Maggie hoped so, because the last thing she wanted to do

was upset Miranda Barrett after everything she'd done for them. Ben's mom had single-handedly planned their entire wedding, which they'd held last winter in Ben's hometown, Cobb Valley. It had been a small but elegant affair. Maggie had never felt more loved and wanted as she'd walked down the aisle toward Ben, the high-pitched jingles of Summer's steel drum accompanying her steps.

They'd honeymooned in Prague, a city Maggie had fallen in love with after visiting Ben on his movie set. They were planning on going back when Maggie took advantage of her vacation time from the community center, but she was in no rush. She loved living in Manhattan, with Ben, in their gorgeous brownstone.

Besides, they couldn't miss the Golden Globes award ceremony, not when Ben was a first-time nominee in the best supporting actor category.

"All done," Greg announced, patting her lower back with a warm cloth to wipe off the excess ink.

She stood up and craned her head, trying to get a glimpse of her back. Both men chuckled, and Greg finally put her out of her misery and ushered her toward the full-length mirror in the main room of the tattoo shop. She examined the tribal design, the soft lines and curved accents making it more feminine than the one on Ben's biceps.

"I love it," she finally announced.

Both men released relieved sighs, which made her realize what a bitch she must have acted like during the hour they'd been here. Too bad. She didn't care what anyone said, tattoos *hurt*.

She and Ben thanked and paid the tattoo artist, then slipped into their winter coats and stepped outside onto the icy city sidewalk. Thanks to the adrenaline coursing through her body after getting inked, Maggie barely felt the frigid wind as it hit her. She gripped Ben's hand and shot him a smile.

"I feel like a bad girl, now that I have a tattoo and all," she said with a grin.

"You *feel* like a bad girl? Uh-uh, you *are* one," he corrected. "Or don't you remember what you did to me after the Golden Globes nomination brunch, on the flight home last week?"

"That was pretty bad, wasn't it?"

"Oh yeah."

They stopped at a crosswalk and waited for the stoplight to change. Maggie wanted to rip off her coat and examine her tattoo again, but she stopped herself. She couldn't believe how her life had changed for the better during the past year. Sure, the press still hounded them every now and then, and lately it was the former, seeing as Ben was up for an award. But aside from that, everything was incredible. Ben made her breakfast every day before she left for work, and at night, she cooked him dinner, then made up for the awful flavorless meal in the bedroom.

"So my mom called yesterday when you were at work," Ben mentioned as they crossed the street.

"Yeah, what'd she want?"

"She wanted to know when she'll be getting a grandchild."

Maggie nearly slipped on the snow-covered sidewalk under her boots. "What'd you tell her?"

"That we're working on it."

"Oh are we?"

"Of course we are." He flashed a magnetic smile. "Aren't you looking forward to it, having a tiny little Ben Barrett running around the house?"

She let out a groan. "Oh God. Two Ben Barretts? The world had better watch out."

"We both know you love me."

He squeezed her hand and she shivered from the familiar tingles his touch evoked in her body. "Yeah, you're right. I guess I do love you."

"You guess?" he said with mock insult.

She grinned. "Fine. I *know* I love you."

And when they got home, she ushered him into the master bedroom and showed him exactly how much.

About the Author

To learn more about Elle, please visit www.ellekennedy.com. Send an email to Elle at elle@ellekennedy.com or visit her blog, the Sizzling Pens, at http://sizzlingpens.blogspot.com.

GREAT
CHEAP
FUN

Discover eBooks!

THE FASTEST WAY TO GET THE HOTTEST NAMES

Get your favorite authors on your favorite reader, long before they're out in print! Ebooks from Samhain go wherever you go, and work with whatever you carry—Palm, PDF, Mobi, and more.

Printed in the United States
148877LV00001B/48/P